DEATH IN COLD PRINT

CONDITIONS OF SALE

DEATH IN
COLD PRINT

JOHN CREASEY

UNABRIDGED

PAN BOOKS LTD : LONDON

First published 1961 by Hodder & Stoughton Ltd.
This edition published 1964 by Pan Books Ltd.,
8 Headfort Place, London, S.W.1

Printed in Great Britain by Richard Clay and Company, Ltd.,
Bungay, Suffolk

CONTENTS

DEDICATION

This book is dedicated to all the printers, in Great Britain and in many parts of the world, who have helped to produce my books and stories.

At every stage of production I have been saved from many a serious slip, and helped beyond measure in spelling, punctuation, and syntax.

To them all, my warm thanks.

I am particularly grateful to Richard Clay and Company, the printers of this book for letting me spend so much time at their works, and for reading and advising on the book even before it got into print.

Anything that is wrong is my fault entirely!

J. C.

1

MAN ALONE

JENSEN began his watch on that clear, starlit evening in March with his spirits higher than they had been for a long time. He was in luck, more luck than a one-armed man with a night-watchman's job could reasonably expect. Doris would be here by eight o'clock or so, it was now half past seven, and on Wednesday evening she was a certainty, because poor old Charlie always went to his pub for a couple of pints and his darts, not dreaming that his wife was going to have her fun, too. If a man of nearly sixty married a girl in her twenties, what else could he expect?

Jensen punched the first of the time clocks, near the main gates, and produced its usual dull, metallic clang. He had twelve clocks to punch, and the complete round of this part of the works would take exactly half an hour. Then he was allowed half an hour's rest in the time-keeper's office; the bosses even allowed him to put his feet up and his head down on a camp-bed in the corner. Very understanding, the R. & K. bosses!

The night-watchman grinned to himself in the gloom of the passages, and walked along to his next stopping place, where the clock was lost in dark shadows. He knew the works inside out, there was hardly an alcove or a recess, a storage bin or a machine which he could not find, even in this eerie light. For years he had been a machine minder on one of the two great rotary presses, fascinated by the electric controls, almost hypnotized by the rhythmic movement and by the humming sound of the mighty machines which could print ten thousand sheets an hour. But a machine minder needed two sound hands and arms. So did everyone doing the kind of job he had wanted to do, and since the night when he skidded on his motor-cycle, he had lost any chance of getting the right kind of job.

He seldom thought about it now, although for months he had been bitter and vengeful about the accident, in some ways feeling worse because he could blame no one else. He had taken a corner too fast on an icy road, skidded and crashed

7

into a telegraph pole. If he was honest with himself, he would admit that he had been lucky to escape with his life. Bess, on the pillion, hadn't. Bonk on the head, no helmet, that had been that. It was a funny thing, but he had never really missed Bess; after all, he had been engaged to her for only three months, and had known plenty of girls before her. He had persuaded himself that Bess was different from the others but hadn't thought much about her when he had come round in hospital. No one had really blamed him for the accident; it was difficult to condemn a man who was in hospital with multiple injuries.

That was all in the past, three years gone. For a year he had been an odd-job man and sweeper, then he had been offered the night-watchman's job, which enabled him to do what he liked most of the day. It didn't pay him a fortune, but he got by. After the first few weeks he had come almost to like the dark corners, the tiny sounds of the night; the stillness and the loneliness.

For the past three months there had been Doris, and a very different mood. He had come in as usual one Friday afternoon, to collect his wages, and Doris, who worked in the bindery, had been there too. They'd known each other casually for years, and she had gone to the same school as Bess— which wasn't really surprising, there being only two schools in Corby. That Friday they had been left alone for a few minutes, Doris had asked him if he wasn't lonely at night, and half jestingly he had said:

'Gets me down, Doris, take it from me. How about coming and keeping me company now and again? Help scare the ghosts away.'

'You'd be lucky,' she had retorted, but something in her expression, a kind of eagerness, had told him that if he pressed a little more she might take him up on the offer.

'Wouldn't do any harm,' he had urged, 'and Old Charlie takes his nights out at the pub, doesn't he?'

'That's about all he's good for,' she had said, and the touch of bitterness had confirmed everything that Jensen had suspected.

'How about it, then, Doris? I've got a snug little place here, we could have a drink and a nice chat—you'd be doing me a good turn, you would really. How about tomorrow? Charlie always goes out Saturdays and Wednesdays, doesn't he?'

8

'You seem to know all about him,' Doris had retorted.

The following evening, just before eight o'clock, she had turned up, a little nervous, a little giggly; but very soon Jensen had realized that she had really wanted exactly the same thing as he, and the R. & K. camp-bed was a pretty firm one.

Doris had taught him a lot, too; Bess hadn't been in it, none of the girls he'd known had been able to excite him in the way that Doris could. Of course, there was always a fly in the ointment; last Friday she had given a hint that it would be wonderful if they could get married. But he could handle that situation all right; after all, Charlie was good for another twenty years.

So Jensen went on his rounds on that chilly Wednesday, in the best possible mood, and with no reason at all to suspect that there would be trouble. He didn't hurry through the yellow-lit shops and passages; thirty minutes was exactly the right time for going round all the departments and looking in all the places where a fire might start, all the danger spots where someone might break in, the dark corners where they could hide. Burglars were the least of his worries, but there had been a couple of tramps in the paper warehouse one night who had given him a nasty turn, and wherever there was a lot of paper, there was always a risk of fire. Every ceiling was fitted with sprinklers, every main doorway had a sprinkler control, and his instructions were crystal clear; if he saw any evidence of fire, use the sprinklers first and then send for the Fire Service and one of the directors. Twice he had seen a faint red glow in the shadows, where cigarettes had been flung down by careless workmen, but he had never needed to use the sprinklers.

He walked through the Composing Room, where thirty machines stood like squat spectres in the grey light from the windows—these were the Monotype setting machines. He went into the casting room, where the faintly astringent smell of molten metal made him wrinkle his nose. He strolled out of this comparatively small room, past complicated machines which seemed to write by themselves, out into the much bigger room where the chases were made up. This covered a huge area. On the dozens of stones, or waist-high tables, were the formes, in each of which pages of books were locked, some only half ready for press, some all ready for machining in the morning.

He punched the clock here, and went next into the largest of all the shops, where the two rotaries and the smaller machines stood, like enormous automatons and their satellites. Here a light on the ceiling spread a pale yellow glow, but he was able to see practically every corner. The smell of printing ink, the hard, smooth smell of paper, and the stink of oil pervaded this vast room, which was a hundred feet wide and nearly a hundred yards long. He walked towards 'his' machine, and stood looking up at it like an acolyte before an altar, then stepped on to the metal ladder and up to the control platform. He always had a kind of choky feeling whenever he stood here on this nightly pilgrimage. He did not realize it, but he loved this machine. He put his hand on the cold metal caressingly, smoothed down the great rolls of paper, and stood there for two or three minutes, everything else forgotten.

Then he heard a car.

Very few cars came down here, because the works lay off the main road, very nearly half a mile from the town of Corby itself. The main gates were locked, and there was no other way of getting a car into the grounds. Sensitive to the slightest thing out of the ordinary, Jensen raised his head and listened. The car seemed to be coming nearer, but suddenly the engine stopped.

He grinned.

'Couple out for a cuddle, that's what that is,' he decided aloud, and soon brought his thoughts back to Doris. He had been dawdling, and he didn't want to keep her waiting. He punched the clock in the Rotary Machine Shop, and went into the equally large shop which housed the smaller flat-bed machines, with the colour-printing jobs at the far end. Everything was normal, there was no hint of smoke. He went more quickly but without haste past the Heath-Robinson-like folding machines, then along the two elongated paper-back binders, over to the normal binding machines. Everywhere were piles of books, some folded, some in sheets, some already bound and ready for dispatch. He passed the two big guillotines, where the book edges were trimmed, great blades poised and silent, but ready to come down with ruthless efficiency at the touch of a switch. Not for the first time, Jensen reminded himself that only a touch of a switch was needed to make this place wake to life.

Now, it was a dead place of gloom and smells and silence.

10

He punched his last clock, and stepped out into the yard which separated this part of the works from the main storage sections, where great stocks of a hundred different kinds of paper, board, cloth for binding, inks, and glues were kept, with the hoists and the pulleys and the modern doors which opened whenever a trolley approached them and fell into place as soon as the trolley was past. The stars were clear but seemed small. There were no clouds. The wind was gentle, not at all cold for March. The huge iron gates were closed, and there was no sign of a car; it would be parked off the road somewhere out of sight, of course.

Doris wasn't there.

He strolled towards the gates, lighting a cigarette; the rule was that he should not smoke except outside, or in the office, and he obeyed this rule absolutely. He could wait outside by the gates, now, or he could go in and unfold the bed. He kept smiling to himself, for his *affaire* had been going on long enough for him to accept it as normal, and to take it for granted that there would be no trouble.

It was funny Doris wasn't here.

He glanced at his wrist-watch; it was five minutes past eight. She knew that he had to start his rounds again at half past, and this was the first time she had been late; she always did one of his rounds with him, and occasionally she liked to push his card into the clock and pull the lever down—necessary in order to prove that he had made the round as he should do. It wasn't that the firm was suspicious of him; it was an insurance company's requirement.

He reached the huge double gates. Built into one of the two sections of the main gate was a small one which he often used, and which was large enough to admit pedestrians and cyclists, but kept cars out. Doris would come along from Corby on her bicycle. He unlocked the gate, and strolled towards the corner of the fence and looked along towards the town. He did not see the car, and saw no sign of Doris's cycle lamp.

'What's keeping her?' Jensen asked himself, and his words seemed to float on the quiet night. He was annoyed, and it was the first time he had ever felt like that with Doris. Then he reasoned that he ought to give her a break. She would come if she could, there was no doubt about that. Anything might have detained her. Old Charlie might have decided to stay in, for instance.

11

'Not much chance of that,' he murmured. He kept peering along the twisting road from the town for fully five minutes, and then turned back to the main gates and the works. He was fed up. She wasn't coming; it was nearly a quarter past eight, he could forget her. He let the small gate clang, and locked it roughly, then turned towards the offices.

He saw a light.

It was not the glow from the low-wattage lamps which were on through the night, it was the brighter beam of a torch.

He thought: 'My God!'

Then he thought: 'She's got in, the little devil, she's managed to get in! She's fooling me.'

He stifled a chuckle and went to the office door, unlocked it with his key, and stepped inside. There was a passage with several offices on either side, and the big wages office on the right. The door was ajar, but now the light was out.

'Stop fooling!' he called. 'I know you're there!'

Doris didn't answer.

'Doris, cut it out,' he called, and pushed the door wider open.

There was just enough light to see by. The folded bed; the big empty desks; the racks where the time cards were kept when they were being checked and the wages computed; the desk lamps, the adding machines, the comptometers – but there was no sign of Doris, and the bright light of the torch had vanished.

'Doris, pack it in,' he called uneasily.

He looked behind the door, but she wasn't there. That was when he began to realize that this wasn't Doris, fooling about; by now she would have revealed herself, they would be laughing and hugging each other. He didn't like the sound of this at all, and he stood in the doorway, looking along the passage, listening intently. He heard nothing. He remembered that car engine, and wondered whether there was any possibility that it had anything to do with this situation.

All he had to do was dial 999 – which would alert the police in Corby. When he had disturbed those tramps he had dealt with them himself, and the bosses had torn a strip off him the next morning; whenever there was the slightest sign of trouble, he had to dial 999, and within five minutes help would arrive. If it proved a wasted journey for the police, no one would mind.

But it *might* be Doris.

'Doris, is that you?' he called again.

There was no answer, but he heard a creak of sound behind him. He spun round. He saw the man, arm raised, weapon poised, and flung up his arm to try to protect himself, but the weapon crashed on to his skull.

He groaned as he crumpled up, and screamed as the second blow came.

2

WOMAN ALONE

DORIS BLAKE knew that she should not be going out to the works, knew how wrong it was, and yet was driven by a compulsion which she could not resist. Sometimes, in the cottage where she and her husband lived alone, she would sit in the little front room with her eyes screwed up and her hands clenched, hating what she had let herself in for. She had been warned time and time again when she had talked of marrying Charlie, that it couldn't work out; that twenty-nine and sixty-three just weren't made for each other. But she had been lonely for so long, and nervous of being left on the shelf; and Charlie was a handsome chap, tall, strong, and good humoured.

She didn't really hate him; she simply longed for freedom.

It wasn't the sex side of the marriage, either, because Charlie was almost undemanding – in fact all he had really wanted was a housekeeper who would make his money go a long way, and keep his cottage as spick and span as his first wife had. His first wife's photograph was in every room, and he would sit back in his big saddle-backed chair, and talk about her and their three children, one in London, one in Canada, one in Australia.

Doris was no picture postcard, she knew, and the funny thing was that no one seemed to realize what a good figure she had – except Jack Jensen.

She was in love with Jack, but wasn't quite sure whether he was in love with her. Last Friday she had almost screwed herself up to the point of saying that whatever happened she would leave Charlie, so that he could get a divorce; but she had resisted the temptation, partly because of Charlie, partly because she wasn't sure of Jack. On Saturday, a wonderful evening, she had hinted at marriage if she could get her freedom, but Jack hadn't taken the hint, although he was pretty quick on the uptake. There was always the danger that he would not want to tie himself down even if he could.

Doris couldn't make up her mind what to do, but was rapidly coming to the conclusion that it would have to be all or nothing. She couldn't keep sneaking off on Wednesdays and Saturdays, spend the evening with Jack, and get home just before Charlie arrived. Charlie knew she had been out, of course; she had gone out on his 'pub' nights ever since they had been married, spending the evening with a friend. May, the friend, knew where she went these days, and didn't approve, but she would be loyal. If there were any questions asked she would say that Doris had been with her.

On the Wednesday evening as Doris waved to Charlie when he went out, she felt her heart beating wildly fast. She would have to bring things to a climax, whether Jack liked it or not. It had been one thing to lose her head as she had done those first few nights, but May was absolutely right, it couldn't go on.

She would have to deliver a kind of ultimatum to Jack; either he must promise to marry her if she could get a divorce, or they must give up the association. She would hate that, but not as much as she hated deceiving the man she had married.

She went back to the little yard at the back, took her bicycle from the shed, and pedalled off. She would visit May for ten minutes, as she always did – that way, she wouldn't have to tell any actual lie. It was a nice evening, the stars were out, and but for the turmoil of her mind she would have enjoyed the ride away from her section of the little town towards May's place. Luckily, May's cottage was near the works, only five minutes' cycle ride away.

May's husband was a merchant sailor, and May spent most of her time in her cottage alone with her three children; one kid every Christmas leave, May would say jokingly. She did not see her husband more than three times a year, yet she lived for him.

The children were in bed.

'Come on in, dear, and have a cup of tea,' May greeted, and the warmth in her voice did Doris good. Doris took the woollen scarf off her head and loosened her tweed coat. 'Isn't it warm for the time of the year, not often we get this kind of weather in March,' May went on. She was a little thing, quite pretty, always bustling. 'I've been thinking a lot about you today, Doris, and I've come to the conclusion that it's not up to me to preach or tell you what to do. It's your own life and you've got to live it your own way. The only thing I ask is, try not to hurt old Charlie too much.'

Try not to hurt old Charlie . . .

When she left the cottage Doris found that phrase echoing in her mind. She went over everything in her married life and tried to be quite honest with herself about it. She was more than ever sure that Charlie was fond of her, but that he didn't really regard her as his wife – not in the sense that he had his first wife. He would lose a housekeeper, but she didn't think that it would *hurt* him, whatever happened. Curiously, now that May had taken this new attitude, she herself felt more strongly than ever that she could not go on deceiving Charlie. It was one thing to walk out on him; another to share his bed, let him support her, and come out twice a week to see Jack.

She cycled away from May's cottage half an hour early, eager to get her burden off her mind. She could see the works as a dark mass against the sky, the roofs just above the high fence. She would not have been able to see that but for the main-gate lamp, because the lights of Corby lay over on the right. The only sound was the purring of her tyres on the smooth road, and a little click-click of the pump, which was rather loose.

There was no doubt she would have to have it out with Jack, tonight. But —

Supposing he refused to marry her? She made herself face that possibility. If he did, what would she do? It was simple to *say* that she would just give him up, but how easy would it be?

As the doubts assailed her, she heard a sound behind her, and then became aware of headlights swaying up and down. Very few cars came along here, and usually it was someone who had lost their way – unless Mr Richardson was making a night visit. He did sometimes, to check that all was well, and she dared not be seen by any of them. She pulled into the side of the road, her heart thumping. They might slow down to see who it was, and even if they didn't they would wonder who was going along this way tonight.

The lights swept upon her, casting her long, black shadow ahead; then the car passed, its engine very loud, tyres making a hissing noise. She saw two men in it, and one of them was looking at her, but she could not see his face properly. She was sure that it wasn't one of the bosses, and this was a small car, too.

Its red lights glowed.

It would soon come to the dead end, and then it would swing back this way, or it might turn down the road past

Soley's Farm, and go back to Corby that way. She saw it swing round towards the farm, and disappear, but the headlights still showed against the sky. There was nothing for her to worry about, anyhow.

Then the lights went out.

Doris frowned into the dark night, which seemed black after that blaze of light in the sky, and pedalled more slowly. She couldn't understand why a car's lights should go out in the country like that – it wasn't as if there had been a man and a girl in the car, it would be easy enough to understand then. She watched the road which led to Soley's Farm, but saw no sign of movement. Her legs moved more and more slowly on the pedals so that the front wheel began to wobble.

She was only a hundred yards from the farm turning, and two hundred yards from the main gates of the works, when she saw the two men leave the car, shadowy figures in the light from the works gates.

She was frightened, but at that time only because she was afraid of being recognized. She stopped, and got off the bicycle. The two men moved across the road and disappeared towards the gates. Possibly they were going to see Jack, and he expected them; it was also possible that they were works employees, engineers doing some maintenance work. Goodness! Charlie was the engineer-shop foreman! But he would have told her if he was going back to the works. She reminded herself again that the important thing was to avoid being recognized. If she turned back she would have no chance of seeing Jack tonight, so she must wait until the couple went off. So anxious was she to keep out of sight that she was prepared to stay this distance away, but then she remembered the footpath from the road to Soley's Farm. She could wheel her bicycle along there, and see the main gates and the works from behind the hedge. She crossed the road. Now that she was accustomed to the night, and was nearer the gates, she would see everything she needed to: the hedge, the works wall beyond it, the works chimneys, and, in the other direction, the lights at the windows of Soley's Farm. She began to wonder if she could have made a mistake, and if the car had gone to Soley's, and past the silo, but suddenly she saw it parked near the field – the gate light shining faintly on the high gloss of the roof.

Doris left her bicycle against the hedge, and walked

17

cautiously towards the car, because she could see the gates from there. She thought she heard voices, and wondered if Jack was talking to the men. She felt her heart palpitating, and wished she had never come tonight, almost wished that she had never become involved with this.

What a night to come early!

There was no sign of Jack or anyone at the gates, and she must have imagined the voices. The direct light from the gate took away something of the eeriness of being alone. She stood holding the handlebars, quite close to the car, wondering what was the wise thing to do. Then she saw the men, climbing over the iron-barred fence on the right. One moment they were clearly visible, the next they dropped down. She heard the thump of their footsteps, saw them steady themselves against the iron bars, and look round towards her. Although she knew that she could not be seen, she felt as if the men knew that she was there. One of them actually raised a hand, as if in a kind of mocking salute. Then they turned and walked together towards the office.

'Jack!' she gasped aloud. 'Jack, they're thieves!' She wanted to shout, but knew that if she did, the men would hear. Other possibilities flashed blindingly through her mind. She could rush to a telephone, there was one not far from May's cottage, and tell the police. Then she realized that she would have to give her name, and would have to explain what she had been doing out here. Nonsense! she told herself desperately. I can telephone the police but needn't say who I am. I can just tell them I saw two men climbing into the works. That's bound to be enough, the police are sure to come!

She gripped the bicycle tightly, and pushed it towards the road – and as she passed the car, and her foot went on to the pedal, she saw a man on the other side of the car.

He leapt at her.

Now for the first time she knew panic. There was the leaping man, his hands outstretched as if to clutch her throat, and she saw his face quite clearly, a small face, a small man, with dark hair and glittering eyes. She hardly knew what she was doing as she jumped away from the bicycle and pushed it towards him. It got in his way. She saw him try to fend it off, but he could not, and staggered back. The bicycle clattered noisily, and its bell went *ting*. She turned and ran, unable to think beyond escaping from the man who was chasing her. She heard the clattering again; the bell kept making that tinging sound, the man was scrambling to his feet. She reached the smooth road itself, where it was easier to run, and looked over her shoulder, gasping. She saw the man running after her, and catching up.

'Jack!' she screamed. *'Jack, help me!'*

The cry faded away; there wasn't a hope that Jack would hear it, and yet it was her only hope.

'Jack, Jack, Jack!' she kept sobbing.

She caught her foot against a stone, and nearly pitched forward. She heard the thudding footsteps of the man behind her, and knew that he was getting nearer. She thought she could hear his breathing. The lights of Corby were so far off that they seemed to come from a different world, and there was no help for her. She looked over her shoulder. The man was only a few feet away, his hands were outstretched again. There was only one hope – to get to the works, to scream for Jack, to make him hear. She swung round, and the man was so surprised that he swung past her. She did not think to put out a leg and try to trip him up, she only gasped:

'Jack, Jack!' and ran wildly.

Then a hand clutched the flying tails of her coat. She was jolted to a standstill, and jerked back. Suddenly, she was pressed against the man, and his hands were round her throat. She kicked backwards and kept flinging her arms about, but she couldn't free herself, and the tightness at her throat became agonizing.

There was pain at her breast and greater pain at her throat; and strange lights – and darkness.

3

SPECIAL REQUEST

'ARE YOU sure you'll be all right?' asked Janet West, on the Thursday morning of the last week in March. 'I've got everything in, I don't think you'll need to buy a thing, and if you should run out of anything, Mrs Clark or Mrs Welling will let you have it.'

'I expect to run out of whisky,' announced Roger West.

'The Clarks would even supply that,' Janet said. She was inches shorter than her husband as they stood in the kitchen of their home in Bell Street, Chelsea, and she was looking up into his eyes, a little uneasily. 'You don't mind me going on ahead, do you?'

Roger laughed, and slid his arms round her shoulders.

'Don't be a goop, of course I don't, and I'll be down with you on Saturday. Forget all about me until then. You're as edgy as if you were leaving the boys for me to look after. That would really be cause for alarm.'

'I half wish they weren't coming with me, they'd keep an eye on you,' Janet said. 'I know it's absurd, but I have a kind of feeling that something will go wrong.'

'Such as the house burning down?'

'Such as you having to go up north on a case when the boys and I are in Bedford,' Janet said.

'There are such things as telephones,' Roger pointed out mildly, 'and jobs in the North Country don't come as often as that. Stop worrying, and concentrate on having a wow of a family reunion. It's only about once every five years that your brother Ralph comes home from the States, and you ought to be jumping for joy because you're going to spend a long weekend at home with him.'

'I am. If only I could be sure that you —'

'I'll be there Saturday at the latest. What time are you leaving?'

'The boys are meeting me at Euston for the one-ten,' Janet answered. 'We'll be at Bedford soon after two. Roger, this might be your last chance to see Ralph – he's only in England for a few days. Why don't you come up now and drive back to London in the morning?'

'Because I'd rather spend the evening clearing up all the odds and ends I can so as to have the whole weekend free without a lot of desk work piling up for Monday morning,' Roger said. 'Jan, I must go, it's after nine, and I won't be at the office until half past.'

'As you weren't home until two o'clock, who's to blame you?'

'It's a peculiar thing,' said Roger, affecting a long-suffering air, 'but policemen's wives never seem to grasp the simple fact that crime and criminals do not work to a time-table.' He gave her a bear hug, let her go, and turned towards the back door. 'I'll be at Bedford tomorrow night,' he insisted. 'Big jobs don't often run in pairs, and now we've got Sparkham in clink I'll be given the odd jobs for a few days, while I'm preparing the case against Sparkham. How about opening the garage doors for me?'

A few minutes after he waved to Janet from the wheel of his car, a black Humber Snipe, and settled down for the twenty-minute drive to Westminster and the Yard. He did not hurry. No one at the Yard would be surprised or censorious if he didn't turn up till midday, for he had had three very late nights in a row. All of these had been while working to trap the jewel thief, Monty Sparkham, who had killed a jeweller in Ealing several weeks ago. Tracing him, tracking him down, and finally arresting him had been quite a job, but it was all over bar the shouting.

Traffic was fairly thick, but not yet at its worst, and Roger turned into the Embankment entrance of the Yard a little before nine-thirty. He was acknowledged by the policeman on duty, parked his car near the steps, and went briskly up them. Last night's arrest had been a stimulant, he wasn't even slightly tired. He looked across at the Cannon Row Police Station, knowing that Sparkham was in the cells there; he would be up at Bow Street about eleven o'clock this morning, and Roger would give evidence of arrest and ask for an eight-day remand in custody. He nodded, smiled, or raised a hand twenty times on his way along the passages and up in the lift to his own small office overlooking the Embankment.

Cope, his chief *aide*, was at a small desk in his shirt-sleeves, although the windows were wide open and a keen wind came off the Thames.

'Morning, Handsome.'

'Morning, Dave. What's new?'

'Well, I dunno how it was managed, but one of our chaps picked up that Sparkham customer last night. Must have been working overtime.'

'Couldn't sleep, I suppose,' said Roger, straight-faced. 'I said what's new, I don't want the old stuff.'

'You work too much, that's your trouble,' said Cope. 'S'matter of fact, Handsome, there isn't much in this morning, and nothing new for you. The usual lot of pros – fat lot o' good the new Act did – couple of raids last night, a few fights, crop of burglaries, and a couple of smash and grabs, but Hardy hasn't sent anything along for you.'

'I hope he keeps it that way,' Roger said. 'If I can get off by three o'clock tomorrow I'll make my wife a happy woman.'

'Only thing that would make my wife happy would be if I worked twenty-four hours a day seven days a week,' grumbled Cope. 'The way she talked to me this morning you'd think I was something that crawled.'

'Find out what time Sparkham's being taken to Bow Street and make sure I get plenty of notice,' Roger said. 'Then get cracking on the outlines of the case for the legal boys. They can have the weekend to chew it over.'

He took off his coat, and ran through reports on several other cases on his desk. The signs were good, there shouldn't be any trouble in taking the weekend off. Apart from pleasing Janet, he wanted to see his brother-in-law; they had been very good friends before Ralph had emigrated just after Roger and Janet's marriage.

At half past ten Cope looked across and announced: 'He's being taken over at eleven-fifteen, should be up at a quarter to twelve.'

'Suits me,' said Roger, and the telephone bell rang at his desk as he spoke. He lifted the receiver. 'West speaking ...' He paused, and asked: 'Where from? ... Corby? Find out the name of the caller, will you?' He closed his hand over the mouthpiece, and said to Cope: 'Where's Corby?'

'Border of Essex and Suffolk, isn't it?'

'Oh, I've got the place,' Roger said, his frown disappearing. 'Who do I know there?'

'Don't ask me the dark secrets of your private life,' said Cope. 'I —'

'It's Superintendent Tenterden,' the operator stated. 'He said that you would remember him.'

'So I do,' said Roger promptly. He closed his hand over the mouthpiece again. 'It's Tenterden who used to be at Colchester. They farmed him out ... Hallo, Mr Tenterden, nice to hear from you again ... What can I do for you?'

The man at the other end of the line spoke slowly and deliberately, and Roger recalled more about him; a slow-speaking East Anglian, a typical flatfoot-to-superintendent type, sound, cautious, unobtrusive, florid-faced – and suddenly Roger remembered that he had an unexpectedly lovely wife.

'I'm sure you won't mind me telling you about my problems, Mr West,' Tenterden said, 'and I thought I would before I made any recommendations to the Chief Constable. The truth is I want some help down here, and you're the man for my money if you're free. If you're tied up for a day or two I'd hang on until you're free – that's if you could swing it either way.'

Roger asked cautiously. 'What's on?'

'Got a nasty murder on our hands, and I don't want to make a hash of it. Very difficult situation for us local chaps, too.' Tenterden's slow manner of speaking made his colloquial phrases seem a little stilted. 'The night-watchman of Richardson and Key, the big printers down here, was murdered last night. Very nasty job, head smashed right in, I've had a look round myself and put my chaps on it, and there'll be someone out from Colchester during the morning. But in my opinion we need someone from the Yard.'

'Why?' asked Roger, and tried to pin-point Corby on the map.

'Well, half the population of Corby works at the printing works or lives off it some way or other,' said Tenterden, 'and I know the lot of them. Went to school with half of them, too – did you know this was where I started? Er —'

He broke off.

Roger found himself thinking: 'I get it,' and felt sure that he understood at least part of the man's motives. Superintendent Tenterden was batting on his own wicket, and it could become a sticky one. If he had to have help it was far better that it should be acknowledged experts from Scotland Yard rather than another, probably younger, local man. Prestige could mean a lot in a small country town. Roger now had a map of Eastern England on his mind's eye. Corby couldn't be more than eighty or ninety miles from Bedford, where Janet's family lived; it would be no more difficult driving there from Corby than driving from London. He could do with a job out of the London area, too; he hadn't been in the country for nearly six months. Once there, he would be his own master; no one could thrust a new job on to him at the last minute.

Tenterden was saying.

'... never quite sure of the form up here, Mr West, but I know my Old Man pretty well, and he'll consult the Yard if I recommend it strongly enough. How *are* you fixed?'

Roger temporized: 'It's not as simple as that, it depends on who the Assistant Commissioner thinks would be best for the job.'

'Oh, you would,' Tenterden said emphatically.

Roger thought: 'Why's he so sure?' All Tenterden needed was a man from the Yard, the individual really couldn't matter.

'You made a big hit when you were on that factory job out at Ipswich,' Tenterden explained, 'and there was that other motor-works job you handled. What I mean is, Mr West, you've had a lot more experience than most in jobs which involve big plants and work-people. Richardson and Key employ nearly a thousand people here, and it would be easy to get in their bad books. That's what I'm afraid of doing, naturally – and if you knew the people we have to deal with down here you'd know they can close up like oysters if they get rubbed up the wrong way. If we fetch someone from Essex police they'll turn up their noses. If they have to put up with me for too long they'll pretend to be sleeping. But if they had you to deal with – well, your reputation would break 'em down.'

Roger chuckled.

'That's enough blarney,' he said. 'I could come down if I got the job, though. Why don't you get moving right away?'

'Will you have a word your end?'

'Yes. What's the score with you, though? Any suspect in mind?'

'Got one or two possibilities, but wouldn't like to put it stronger,' said Tenterden, and he seemed to perk up. 'You could come down right away, could you?'

'Sometime today.'

'Tell you what I'll do. I'll send a teletype report up, giving you all the details I can,' said Tenterden. 'One of the funny things is that nothing's missing, as far as we can find out. No damage was done, either – the chap was just battered to death. To make it worse, he'd only got one arm, lost the other in a motor-cycle accident three years ago. Well, thanks, Mr West. Goodbye.'

'Goodbye,' Roger said, and replaced the receiver.

As he did so, he saw Cope leaning forward, elbows on his desk, hands clasped beneath his double chin.

'So you want a nice slack time so that you can go and extend the hand of friendship to your long lost brother-in-law from the United States of America,' he remarked witheringly. 'You sly old so-and-so.'

'That's right,' Roger said. 'I work too hard, remember? The only way I can get time off is by simple cunning. Look up the map – London to Corby, Corby to Bedford, for me, will you? I'm going over to watch Sparkham wishing he could cut my throat.'

He put on his coat, slapped on his hat, and went out.

At Bow Street, Sparkham was remanded for the required and regulation eight days, and Roger negotiated Covent Garden trucks and laden porters as he drove straight back to the Yard. Before going to his office, he went to see the Assistant Commissioner, Hardy. Hardy had come up from the ranks, and could be difficult, but Roger seldom found him so. Now he was sitting at a big desk in a big office: a solid man, not fat and not really big, with iron grey hair, iron grey eyes, and stubby hands with broad but well-shaped finger-tips.

'Just the man I wanted to see,' he greeted. 'Get what you wanted at Bow Street?'

'Yes, thanks.'

'Feel like an out-of-town job?'

'It depends,' said Roger cautiously.

'You can have it or leave it,' Hardy said. 'You've been working your guts out lately, and it's time you eased up. You can stay here and look after the Sparkham case, or you can leave that to Cope and the others, and go down to Corby, in Essex. There's a murder down there they don't want to handle themselves, some kind of wheels within wheels. I don't yet know exactly what. The Chief Constable asked for you if you were free, because it's a factory job. Printing works, rather. You

25

seem to be getting quite a name for yourself as an industrial specialist.'

'Sounds interesting,' Roger said blandly. 'Provided you don't mind if I nip across to Bedford for the weekend – I told you about my wife's brother, didn't I? – I'd like to have a crack at this.' He paused until Hardy said, 'That's all right,' then went on in a brisker voice: 'Wonder when they take men on at the works? Every day, or just on Mondays? And come to think, we ought to have Pratt and Asterley on this job. Pratt did that paper-warehouse investigation last year, and Asterley was on the printing job out at Kingston. They both took jobs, and passed as genuine. Will it be all right to send them down there?'

Hardy laughed.

'Take any two or three you like.'

'Thanks,' said Roger, and glanced at his watch; it was a quarter past twelve. 'I'll get it all laid on, send them down by train, and drive down with Brown. Should be there by about four o'clock. Will you call them at Corby, or shall I?'

'I'll telephone the Chief Constable at Colchester, and he can tell Corby,' answered Hardy. 'Report in once a day, and don't let anyone crack that thick skull of yours.'

That was the nearest that Hardy ever came to making a joke.

By half past one Roger was driving towards Essex, with Detective Inspector Brown sitting next to him. Detective Sergeants Asterley and Pratt were on their way by train, and would apply for jobs at Richardson and Key's works first thing next morning.

Brown was a big, burly, over-weight man with a good mind for detail and a most retentive memory. He was a jack-of-most trades, and his bag contained everything they would need for on-the-spot checks of finger-prints, ballistics, and general work. Brown would give a spot opinion on a dozen subjects, and experts would usually confirm his opinion. He preferred working in the background, too.

'I know you want to have a look at this works before it closes tonight,' he said, as they drove through the suburbs, 'but don't scare the wits out of me.'

'Am I going too fast?' Roger asked, surprised. 'Sorry.' He checked his speed, remembered that Brown was an over-nervous passenger, and waited until they were on the open road before he said: 'Read that teletype message from Corby again, Browny, and don't rush at it. I want to make sure I've got it off pat before I talk to the chaps at Corby.'

'Nothing like proving you're on the ball,' remarked Brown. 'Well, the murdered man's name is Jensen, Jack Jensen. Aged thirty-one, single . . .'

Roger listened intently.

'. . . no apparent motive, nothing stolen, no damage done,' Brown concluded. 'But you don't crack a man's skull for the sake of it, do you? Looks as if this was a pretty strong personal motive, someone hated his guts. Be a nice job, finding which one it was out of nine hundred and forty-three employees.'

'It might have been someone outside the factory, remember,' Roger said musingly. 'Right, thanks. Now hold tight, I'm going to tread on it. This road's safe for seventy.'

4

CORBY

CORBY LAY in the folds of some gentle hills, not far from
the sea, which lay beyond the small fields and the wooded land.
The roofs of the town were old and made of red tiles, mostly
lichen-greened, and mostly made at the ancient tile and brick
works on the outskirts of the town. The main street was wide,
and at the middle wide enough for a coach and eight to turn
in comfort, and the archway of the Rose and Crown, a coach-
ing inn which had been built four hundred years ago, was
spacious enough for two carriages to pass. Inside, the courtyard was cobbled and there were hanging plants of ivy and
geranium and wistaria.

The other streets were narrow, and many of them on the
slopes of the hills. Old cottages, sometimes rows of them with
crooked roofs, had an atmosphere which did not seem to have
been disturbed for centuries, but the windows of many of the
shops were new, and television and radio, new cars and con-
temporary furniture, crowded the shop windows next to but-
chers with the hanging sign: PURVEYORS OF MEAT FOR 300
YEARS.

Roger saw Superintendent Tenterden in the square, near its
old wooden hall, which looked as if a strong wind would blow
it down. Tenterden was six feet two, with a matching girth
and matching shoulders. As he came to greet Roger, Brown
got out of the car; here were two men of equal size and
stature. They all appraised each other as they shook hands.
Tenterden said formally that it was good of the Yard men to
come so quickly, and the people in the square, the shops, and
the streets turned to look at the three men with open curiosity.
Roger, just six feet, was broad and big, but not an ounce over-
weight; compared with these two, he seemed lean. He had
corn-coloured hair which disguised the few streaks of grey, and
his clean-cut features deservedly earned him the nickname
'Handsome'. He was aware of the scrutiny and the curiosity,
and asked Tenterden:

'Have you spread the glad tidings that we're due?'

28

'Just dropped a hint,' said Tenterden. He had a very heavy jowl and rather heavy eyelids, and was even more florid-faced than Roger remembered him, with a tiny criss-cross of purple veins on his nose and cheeks; the heavy-drinker type to look at. 'You said you'd like to go straight out to the scene of the crime, didn't you?'

'Yes. What time do they stop work?'

'Five's knocking off time, but they're busy at the moment, most of the departments will be working until six. Coming in my car, or like to use yours?'

'You take us, will you?' asked Roger.

Tenterden's was an old Rover, and it was a tight fit inside.

'It's about a mile to the works gates, down Factory Road,' Tenterden said. 'The road doesn't lead anywhere else, most of the cottages on either side of it are owned by Richardson and Key, and let off at very reasonable rents to the employees.'

'A good firm to work for?'

'Funny thing to ask, really,' Tenterden said. 'No one else down here would think of asking it. You see, Mr West, this *is* a good place to work and live, and R. & K.'s keep it going. Family firm, you know, been here for over two hundred and fifty years. Know how these East Anglian printing firms started, don't you?' They had driven along a narrow cobbled street into a fairly wide road with small, red-brick Victorian cottages on either side, one or two pubs and shops, and a narrow pavement. 'Dutch and Belgian printers were driven over the North Sea for printing Bibles and heretical literature three hundred years or so ago, and a lot of them settled here. Dozens of big printers and dozens more little ones have been gobbled up by the big 'uns.'

'Interesting,' Roger said formally. 'Slow down a minute, will you?' They were not far from the big iron gates of the works. Three tall chimneys showed up stark against the blue sky, and the throb of machinery came clearly. A big lorry with the R. & K. monogram on its sides came tearing out of the gateway, and had to swing to one side to pass the policemen.

'Young Tom Cousins at it again,' Tenterden remarked. 'I'll have to have a word with Mr Richardson about him. What was it you wanted?'

'Can I get up those chimney stacks to get a bird's eye view of the whole works? I can get my bearings better when I see a plan, then.'

'I daresay,' said Tenterden consideringly. His face cleared. 'But Ben Soley's silo is a much better spot, though. It's higher than any of the chimneys, and easier, too. One of his cow hands fell off it last year and he had a platform put round it to make sure no one else did. Just down here.' He turned left, and they found themselves in a country lane, with fields on one side and a high brick wall on the other. After about a mile, the silo showed up, a big concrete erection with the platform round the top, and iron rungs at the sides for climbing up. No one else was near. Tenterden unhooked a five-barred gate and they stepped into a field of grass and clover which looked as if it had wintered well. 'Dunno that I've got the figure to climb that,' Tenterden added.

'Nor me,' said Brown.

'I'll go,' Roger said. 'Won't be five minutes.'

He went up, cautiously at first, and then more nimbly. The silo was at least sixty feet high, and when he was half-way up he felt the wind more strongly, and the round tower seemed to sway. There was an odour of rotting vegetation, and he kept wrinkling his nose. Then he reached the platform, hauled himself up, waved to the two men who looked so far below, and studied Richardson and Key's works. The odour had become a stench up here.

He had known the works was big; he hadn't realized how big. In some ways it was deceptive, because there were two-storey buildings, and many a factory with half the ground space of this was in fact larger, but the impression was of vastness. There were two distinct sections: on his right, about a dozen low buildings, all with triangle-shaped roofs, and with a lot of window space; on his left, smaller but higher buildings, with three factory chimneys giving off a pale-grey smoke. He saw the masses of cycles, and about a hundred cars, most of them small, parked near the main gates. Close to these gates were red-brick buildings, two or three storeys high, which he imagined to be the offices. There was a covered way between these and some of the low-roofed buildings.

He registered all this on his mind's eye, then walked round the platform and began to descend. He was half-way down, holding on very tightly and feeling that slight swaying movement, when he saw something fluttering from the top edge of the silo; a piece of paper or cloth had got caught, but he couldn't identify it from here. It did not seem to have any significance. A loud tractor engine sounded as he neared the foot of the silo, and he glanced round and saw a farm tractor draw up, with a small, wizened man at the wheel.

This man was saying: 'Now what's your game, Arthur? I didn't put that silo up so as the police could do their PT on it.'

'Afternoon, Sam,' Tenterden said comfortably. 'Mr West of the Yard is just taking a look at the country. It's cheaper than an aerial view.'

'Cost you a pint next time we meet at the Rose and Crown,' said the wizened man.

'I daresay I can go to that,' said Tenterden. 'Mr West, I'd like you to meet Mr Sam Soley, who owns the farm and most of the land round here. And this is Chief Inspector Brown, of Scotland Yard, Sam.'

There were handshakes all round.

'Nasty business over at the works,' Soley remarked. 'Can't say I envy you your job, Mr West, but I hope you find the devil soon. Got anyone in mind yet?'

'I've been here for about half an hour,' Roger answered.

'Thought you Yard chaps solved cases with a wave of the hand,' said Soley, and winked at Tenterden. 'Well, seeing that I'm here I'll go up and have a look at the stuff in the silo, should be nice and ripe by now. Good luck, gents.' He turned away from his machine and began to climb up the iron rungs with much more agility than Roger. The policemen got back into Tenterden's car, and drove towards the works. Roger noticed some broken glass just off the road, and there were tracks of tyres on a patch of soft earth. He caught sight of something else, half hidden by grass near the broken glass, and said:

'Stop a minute, will you?'

Tenterden stopped smoothly, almost alongside the glass.

'That looks like a bicycle pump,' Roger said. He did not see any significance in that, but it was unusual, and it was close to the scene of the night's crime; the murderer might have come along here on a bicycle. 'Let's have a look,' he added, and opened the door and stepped out.

At close quarters there was much more to see.

The glass had been trodden into the ground, and he judged that there was about enough to make up a bicycle lamp. The grass showed no traces of tyres, but there were cycle-tracks some distance away, leading from a hedge, and the path along-

31

side the hedge looked as if it were used a great deal. He saw the heel-prints of a woman's shoes, and strolled towards these, while the other two joined him.

'Looks as if a woman wheeled her bicycle along here, and then let it fall,' reasoned Brown.

Roger said: 'Could be.'

'If she was walking there, how'd the lamp get broken?' asked Tenterden thoughtfully. It was not an effort to assert himself, he was simply speaking his mind. 'The bike must have fallen down with a bump to break the glass and knock the pump out.' He narrowed his eyes and peered along the hedge. 'Looks as if she came off the road by the gate, but what did she stick so close to the hedge for? Much more comfortable cycling along the road.'

'Didn't want to be seen,' Brown suggested.

They turned back towards the road and the car tracks, and after a few seconds Roger said:

'We'd better have this cordoned off, Super — ' He stopped abruptly, grinned, and asked: 'Prefer to be informal?'

'Arthur'll do me.'

'You know what they call me!'

'Browny'll do me,' said Brown.

'Better have it cordoned off, and get a couple of your chaps to look along that path and on the other side of the hedge,' said Roger.

'Can't expect much from the road. It's been used by about nine hundred people, in buses, cars, and on bikes,' declared Tenterden. 'But I'll lay everything on from the office,' and went back to the car.

As he reached it, someone shouted, and all three turned round. Soley was on the platform at the top of the silo, waving and beckoning. He shouted again.

'What's he say?' demanded Brown.

'Let's go and find out,' Roger said, and went at the double towards the silo, while Tenterden and Brown got into the car and began to swing it round.

32

5

SECOND BODY

ROGER PUT his hands to his mouth, and shouted: 'What have you found?'

Soley was leaning over the rail of the platform, one hand at his mouth, and he bellowed back:

'There's a woman's body in here!'

'I'll come up!' Roger called. The car drew alongside, and he stepped to it. 'Arthur, will you get that corner cordoned off, we've got to make sure that too many workers don't walk over it when they come out at five o'clock. Then fix a fire-brigade unit, will you? Soley says there's a body in that silo, and we want to get it up as soon as we can.'

'God!' exclaimed Tenterden. 'Man's?'

'A woman's.'

'I'm going up,' said Tenterden decidedly. 'I might know who it is. Take my car, Browny, will you? I told everyone at the station to take your instructions.'

Brown hesitated until Roger nodded; then Brown turned briskly to the car. Roger let Tenterden start to climb up the silo, and said to Brown *sotto voce:* 'Get back to that corner as quick as you can. Ask the works to lend you some men to put up a barrier so that the crowd can't trample everywhere.'

'Right.' Brown glanced up at Tenterden's huge rear, and went on in a low-pitched voice: 'Think he expected more trouble?'

'Could be.'

'He was certainly in a hell of a hurry to make sure we came down,' Brown said, as if a little put out. 'Not trying to take us for a ride, is he?'

'He's trying to make sure that he won't be blamed for whatever goes wrong,' said Roger. 'And who are we to complain if we get on to a job quickly? Usually everything's as cold as mutton before we get near it.'

'Daresay you're right about Tenterden,' Brown said, without conviction. 'Wonder who the woman is?'

Five minutes later, Roger, Tenterden, and Soley were looking down into the silo, which was no more than a quarter full.

33

Roger disliked the stench intensely, but did not let it put him off. The woman was lying on her back, her legs in a peculiar distorted position, one underneath her, the other bent so that the knee pointed upwards. Her arms were spread out, one hand was tight against the side of the silo. She wore a grey tweed coat, as far as he could judge – it might be a dark blue or a dark green. One shoe was on, one shoe was missing. She looked as if she were asleep down in those shadows, and until they could examine the body it would be impossible even to guess how she had died.

'Not much doubt she was hauled up here, and tossed over,' Soley said.

'Won't be any help to try to examine the body down there,' said Roger. 'No one got down there to kill her, so she was killed up here, or over there.' He glanced towards the spot where he had seen the bicycle pump, and a kind of picture began to form in his mind. 'Recognize her, Arthur?'

'I wouldn't like to swear to it from here, but I think it's a woman named Doris Blake. Her husband's an old pal of mine.' Tenterden seemed almost to be talking to himself. 'Married a girl half his age a few years ago. Never got over his first wife's death, really. Hmm. Well, it won't take long to get her up and find out what happened to her.' He looked intently at Roger, giving the impression that there was something else he wanted to say, but that Soley's presence prevented it. 'If you don't make it soon, you won't see the works before most of the employees start leaving.'

'It'll have to wait,' Roger said. 'Let's have a look at that piece of cloth.'

He was telling himself that he must be slipping, or he would have checked that fragment of fluttering fabric when he had been up here before. Tenterden got it off a rivet which stuck out and had a rough edge. It had been torn from a coat, and was the same colour as the coat on the dead woman.

A police car arrived with two of Tenterden's men, who reported that the fire escape was on its way, with the tackle needed to raise the body. The men, both young and eager, obviously knew their job, and Roger was a great believer in letting younger men and local men feel that they were being given their head. So he let Tenterden drive him to the works, and reached there as a hooter went for five o'clock. A few girls and several men appeared almost on the instant, and he could imagine what it would be like when all the plant's departments closed at the same hour. By the time he reached the office at least two hundred people were surging forward, but the corner where the bicycle had fallen had been roped off, and there was no danger of the tyre tracks and other clues being destroyed.

A tall, very pale and youthful-looking man with thick-lensed glasses and gingery hair stood up from a desk in a small office opposite a much larger one, with the word MANAGING DIRECTOR on the door. He had a twitch at his right eye, gave the impression of being very nervous, and spoke jerkily, as if he could not get the words out quickly enough.

'Ah, Superintendent, so you've arrived. Rather late, I fear, but half the works will be working until six. Very busy. We have part of a very big overseas text-book order to complete next week,' he added, and glanced at Roger. 'Are you Superintendent West?'

'This is Mr West, sir,' said Tenterden. 'Mr West, I asked Mr Sydney Richardson if he could take you round himself. Mr Richardson is the Works Managing Director.'

'Glad to assist,' said Richardson. 'Shocking business. Poor Jensen. To die of violence. And nothing missing, nothing.' He looked at Roger, rubbing his hands together. 'Isn't that remarkable?'

'All murder is remarkable, sir,' Roger said formally.

'Yes, of course. Well, tell me what you want, I'll try to oblige. The Superintendent here has been very helpful. Very. We had to use the other door to the office, poor Jensen was killed in that doorway. Most difficult, you'll agree, not to use the office freely. This is the day before the wages are made up. However, we moved the machines and cards to a temporary office. This one hasn't been used much today. I hope that it can be by tomorrow. Very difficult to make up the wages in any other room.'

'We'll try to get through,' promised Roger.

He saw the camp-bed in the corner, the now empty desks, the card racks, the windows overlooking the yard, and the chalk marks showing where Jensen's body had been found. Obviously the man had been crumpled up. There were some brown stains on the floor, on the door, and on the legs of one of the tables, all marked round with chalked circles. There was no doubt that the local police had been through this room

35

thoroughly; there were all the indications – grey powder tests for finger-prints, chalk marks in several places, little plastic envelopes pinned or Scotch-taped into position, obviously containing hairs, dirt, or small objects which the police thought might be of use in the investigation. A detailed plan of all this was in the making.

'Haven't got much,' said Tenterden. 'Few hairs from the bed, but we haven't unfolded it yet. They were at the side. Cigarette butts, some match-ends, a few crumbs and dozens of finger-prints.'

'I must say, it isn't reasonable to expect all the staff here to have their prints taken,' Richardson said uneasily.

'Isn't it, sir?'

'Surely not.'

'The only way we can find out if there are any prints which shouldn't be here is to find out which ones should,' said Roger. 'Any prints taken with the co-operation of your staff would be destroyed immediately the case was solved, and would not be recorded except for the duration of the case. Do you expect the staff to raise objections?'

'No, no, certainly not,' said Richardson hastily. 'But – *is* it really necessary?'

'I should think so, sir.'

'Tomorrow?'

'Or tonight.'

'No, really! It's twenty past five. In ten minutes the office staff goes home.'

'How many use this office?' inquired Roger.

'Very difficult to say.' Richardson seemed to love the word. 'Difficult matter altogether, so many of the workmen and women come here, of course, on wage queries. That kind of thing. You don't intend to take *all* finger-prints, do you?'

'It might be advisable, sir,' said Roger, and saw another reason why Tenterden had been so anxious to get the Yard's help immediately; he would find it heavy weather with this man, for one.

'But it would cause serious dislocation of the works. And we are very rushed, very rushed indeed.'

Roger said quietly: 'The man Jensen isn't in any hurry now, sir.'

Richardson stopped blinking, just stared, and then said abruptly:

'No. I'm sorry. Must help you all we can.'

'You can be sure that we won't cause any more inconvenience than we have to, sir,' said Roger formally, 'and we don't relish the task of taking everyone's finger-prints any more than you do. We hope we won't have to. What I would like is a quick look round the works, especially to see where Jensen went last night – I understand that he'd had time to do one complete round of the main section of the works, but not the warehouses for storage.'

'That's right, yes. Come along, and I'll take you round. Are you coming, Tenterden?'

'Think perhaps I'd better, sir,' said Tenterden. He gave Roger another of those knowing looks, and went on: 'Many hands been off work today?'

'Very few, very few indeed,' answered Richardson. He glanced at Roger. 'Among my tasks is that of personnel officer, nothing like a personal touch with the work-people. Any special reason for asking, Mr Tenterden?'

'Just like to know of anything unusual.'

Roger thought: 'Our Arthur's a sly old fox.' Then he took advantage of this opportunity to remark:

'As you had only one night-watchman in a works this size, sir, I wondered if you had staff shortages.'

'Sometimes. Never had more than one night-watchman, never been any need,' Richardson answered. 'We never keep much money at the works – it's taken to the bank every night, and collected every morning.'

'Thank you,' Roger said.

They started their rounds. Richardson didn't answer Tenterden's question at first, and it looked as if he were going to evade it; but as they reached the Keyboard Room, where every one of the Monotype machines was being manned by a quick-witted operator, with its big keyboard and the little spool joggling all the time. 'No one in the Keyboard Room here, no one downstairs, all the machine shops were at full complement,' Richardson said abruptly. 'Two engineers, one labourer, one reader, two girls from the bindery, two men from the warehouses, that's the total of absentees.'

'Who were the girls?' asked Roger.

Richardson glanced at him uneasily. 'A Nellie Williams and Doris Blake.'

37

'Thank you, sir,' said Tenterden, and they reached the first of the clocks which Jensen had used every night.

Richardson called the chargehand. Roger asked if anything at all unusual had been noticed when the staff had first arrived, and was assured that everything had been normal. The tap-tap-tap of the keyboards went on all the time; it was as noisy as being in a room with a dozen typists. Next door, the smell of molten metal was very strong, and the attendants were keeping a watchful eye on their machines. Roger found himself watching the bright silvery letters emerging from the complicated mechanism, and suddenly making up a line of print, but he did not pay these particular attention. They went through all the shops, and in some the roar of the machines was almost deafening. Two great rotaries were whirling round at unbelievable speed, and no one here took any notice of the newcomers.

One elderly man gave the same answers about the time clock in that room.

In the sewing and binding rooms hundreds of girls in white smocks and white caps were all doing their job swiftly and mechanically. Here and there was a little party, standing together and talking and laughing, completely unembarrassed by Richardson's presence.

These were watching a long machine which was attaching the brightly coloured covers to paper-back books when one of Tenterden's men came hurrying, and for the first time everyone seemed to stop, every eye was turned towards the detective. Tenterden stood still.

'What is it, James?'

'Thought you'd better know, sir, you were right about the identity of the second body.'

Richardson gasped: '*Second?*'

'That's right,' said Tenterden, and rubbed his big jowl; Roger thought that he looked really distressed, although he tried to hide it. 'Nearly through here now,' he added, and they went on through the doorway which Jensen had used last night. Outside, he stopped, and went on: 'All right for me to take Mr West into the Engineering Shop, sir?'

'Yes, of course,' Richardson said, and his eyes seemed to bulge. 'Machine shop. What are you telling me, Mr Tenterden? Are you going to see anyone in particular?'

'Yes, sir. Charlie Blake.'

'Is that second—?' Richardson broke off.

'Afraid it's Doris Blake, sir,' said the Corby superintendent. 'I thought if we looked through the Engineering Shop on our way, so to speak, we could just have a word in passing with Charlie.'

Richardson said: 'Doris *Blake*. Why, she's worked here since she was fifteen.'

Yes, thought Roger, everyone belongs here. For the first time he felt a surge of annoyance with Tenterden, comprehending what Brown had suspected from the first. Tenterden was virtually taking charge, and yet operating under the cover of the two men from the Yard. He was doing exactly what he wanted to do, putting inquiries in hand without first asking Roger if that was the way he wanted the investigation to go, or if he agreed. It might become necessary to check him, but Roger let it pass this time. Richardson looked even more pale and nervous, and kept repeating the girl's name.

It was Tenterden who opened the big Engineering Shop, with its lathes, its turning machines, its long benches with the racks of tools above them, the heavy odour of oil, and the sharp odour of metal which had just been worked.

Sitting in a small office which was partitioned off from the main shop was a handsome, grey-haired man, who was staring at them. Even at that distance, of thirty or forty feet, it was easy to see that he was red-eyed and pale looking; in fact, he seemed ill. He rose from his stool as the three men approached, and Roger was quite sure that he was sending Tenterden a silent appeal.

'Don't say a word to him yet, except about the time clock,' Roger said. 'I'd rather talk to him when he's alone.'

Tenterden nodded, and they went forward.

6

SUSPECT

CHARLIE BLAKE'S eyes were the eyes of a man with a load of worry on his mind, of a man who had not slept. There were lines of tension at his mouth, pulling down the well-shaped lips. Making allowances for this, he was exceptionally good-looking, and of really distinguished appearance, rather like a film actor playing the part of an engineer. He was tall, his hair was silvery white and plentiful, and it was crimped enough to be attractive without being effeminate. His skin was unusually clear for a man in his sixties.

When the three men entered the Engineering Shop he was sitting down at his desk. He stood up and came towards them. Beyond him, fastened to cup hooks round the walls, were sheaves of paper, obviously time-sheets, notes of instructions, and orders for materials. The little office was very tidy, and so was the desk. After that one long, pleading look at Tenterden, he spoke to Sydney Richardson.

'Good evening, sir,'

'Hallo, Charlie,' Richardson said. 'This is Mr West of Scotland Yard. He wants to know if you noticed anything unusual in the shop this morning, especially at the time clock.'

'No, I can't say I did,' said Blake. He had a pleasant speaking voice, with less pronounced local accent than Tenterden. 'It was going as usual. The card hadn't been stamped, mind you.' He moved towards the time clock, which was at one side of the office, and took out a card from a rack on the wall nearby; every clock had its card rack, and mechanism to register each of the night-watchman's visits.

'Anything wrong at all?' asked Richardson.

'No, sir, nothing unusual,' said Blake. 'They had that bit of trouble on the guillotine this morning. We had a two-hour stand-off on that, but we've had it before.'

'Everything else normal?'

'Yes, sir.'

'Thanks,' said Roger, and led the way out of the Engineering Shop and towards a big paper warehouse, a maze of passages running among great stacks of flat paper which stretched high above their heads. Big hoists and trolleys were stored at one end of this warehouse. There were other warehouses with fat rolls of paper, sheds containing inks and general stores; and none of the time clocks in the warehouse section had been stamped.

They were back at the main offices when a siren blew. Almost instantaneously a dozen or so girls and several men appeared from doorways, and began to line up at the time clocks near the main gates, to stamp their cards. By the time Roger and the others reached the wages office a hundred people were waiting, and the clocks were going *ting, ting, ting.*

'Is there anything else I can do for you?' asked Sydney Richardson. 'I'm at your disposal, Superintendent.'

'Nothing more now,' Roger said, 'but I'd like to be sure by the morning that nothing is missing and that no damage was done.'

'What kind of damage?'

Roger said: 'I don't know. I'd just like to be sure that nothing happened here last night that you haven't discovered.'

'I don't understand you,' Richardson said jerkily. 'We would know, I assure you.'

'Thinking of the guillotine?' asked Tenterden.

'I suppose that put it in my mind,' agreed Roger.

'We have breakdowns frequently,' Richardson said. 'Some minor, some major. It is some time since the big guillotine was out of order, but it is used a great deal, Superintendent, there must be allowances for wear and tear. That is why we keep a large staff of engineers.'

'Was the guillotine all right the night before?'

'Presumably.'

Roger said rather sharply: 'I think that ought to be checked, Mr Richardson. We know that one and possibly two men broke into the premises last night and murdered the nightwatchman, and we want to try to find out if there is any motive connected with this factory, or whether the crimes have a personal motive. Who would be able to tell us about the guillotine?'

'I see your point,' conceded Richardson. 'The chief operator, a man named Malloy, has gone home – I saw him drive past just now. His deputy is in charge. Malloy and Blake would be the most likely men to tell you what caused the trouble with the guillotine. Most unfortunately, everything has been set aside so as to complete the African text-book order, but ...' He changed the subject abruptly. 'If you would like Malloy's address —'

'I know it, thanks,' said Tenterden.

'Then I needn't worry you again tonight, Mr Richardson,' Roger said. 'We'll be working in the wages office and searching the whole works by night, so I don't think you need worry about a night-watchman until tomorrow.'

'Very well,' said Richardson. 'I arranged for two of our part-time workers to come back, but if you don't require them —'

'No reason why they shouldn't come,' Roger said.

Then a pleasant-looking middle-aged woman appeared, and said: 'Sir Lancelot is on the telephone, sir.'

'My partner is in London,' Richardson explained. 'I arranged for him to call me at this time. He is anxious to know if there is any information about the murder.'

'No more, yet,' said Roger. 'Be very guarded in anything you have to say, please.'

'I will be guarded,' Richardson promised stiffly, and turned round. As he did so, a door which appeared to communicate with another office opened, quite sharply, and a girl appeared. She seemed taken aback to find Richardson so close, but Roger saw more than momentary surprise in her expression; he saw concern. The first glimpse showed him that she was tall, slim, nicely built, and very fresh in appearance; the English county type. She wore a white linen blouse and a green skirt with a broad black belt, her hair was rather fluffy, and brushed straight back from her forehead. Even at the first glimpse, Roger noticed her beautifully clear blue eyes.

Like Richardson's.

'Sorry, Daddy,' she said. 'I wondered if you were coming home yet.'

'I shall be a little late tonight, I'm afraid,' Richardson said stiffly. 'Apologize to your mother for me. I will be home in time for dinner.' He gave the girl a mechanical smile; she was obviously troubled by the message and his manner, but said nothing. She glanced from him to the others, as if expecting an introduction, but Richardson went on: 'You get along home. No need for you to stay.'

He went into the office beyond this one, almost pushing his

daughter in front of him, and closed the door on Roger and Tenterden.

Tenterden was looking thoughtfully at Roger as the door closed.

'Nice-looking girl,' Roger remarked. 'Did I hear her say "Daddy"?'

'Yes. She's Rose, Richardson's only child. One of the best,' Tenterden added. 'Best-liked girl in Corby, without exception.'

Roger could have asked: 'What's she worried about?' but didn't. He wasn't sure what Tenterden was getting at, what was in his mind. But he knew that Blake had been in anguish, that he hadn't reported that his wife had been missing all night – and that she had died by strangulation.

What else did Tenterden know about Blake and the people here?

Roger pictured Richardson's daughter again. She had opened the door very quickly, almost impatiently, as if on edge to find out what they had been talking about.

The way she had looked at her father told of real anxiety.

Rose Richardson was certainly anxious about her father, and in a way she had a guilt complex about it, because until the big strike some time ago she had simply taken him for granted. Before then, school in England, a finishing school in Paris, tennis, riding, dancing, spending a lot of time in London, had filled her life, and her father had been a 'funny old thing, but rather sweet'. Her mother had been, too, in a different way – placid, patient, undemanding, proud of her husband and her daughter.

The change in her father after the strike had shocked Rose into talking about him to her mother.

'He's too conscientious, dear,' Mrs Richardson had said. 'It's been his weakness ever since I've known him. If anything goes wrong he always blames himself.'

'But he couldn't blame himself for a nation-wide strike, surely. Practically every printing firm was affected, all over the country.'

'It was the worst I can remember,' agreed Mrs Richardson, 'but your father never believed our men would come out, it was a great shock to him. Rose, you know he'd like you to help out at the office for a few months. Why don't you? Then you might find out if there's anything special worrying him.'

43

'Can't you be sure that something is?'

'No,' Mrs Richardson had answered. 'He's always been nervy and over-zealous, that's really the word, and the strike was such a blow to him. But he's got so bad, I'm really worried about him.'

Rose was, too – now much more than ever; and taking a job as his personal assistant had been the obvious way to try to help.

She knew that her father still slept badly, and that what little sleep he did get was due to drugs which Dr Arnold gave him. The nervous movement of his hands and the twitch at his right eye became worse. They seemed a clear indication of deep anxiety which neither she nor her mother yet understood.

Rose had known the factory all her life as 'the works', and knew the office and some of the departments well, knew and was known by many of the workers, but it wasn't until she began to work on the welfare and personnel side that she understood the complexity of the business, of the plant itself, or the intricacy of the work. For a while she had wondered if it were not simply overwork which was worrying her father, but now she had no doubt at all that something went much deeper.

The Richardsons lived in a converted farmhouse about three miles east of Corby, and nearer the sea. It was on rising ground, with a view of much of the surrounding countryside, and it was possible to see the tops of the chimneys in the factory grounds, as well as the top of Soley's silo. She did not know anything about the finding of the body in the silo, although on her way home she saw the policemen working outside it, and wondered why they were so interested in that particular spot. She swung off the narrow road towards the farmhouse, left her car – an old red MG – and went briskly towards the front door, which stood ajar. Her mother came hurrying; there was no need to wonder what was in her mind.

'How is he taking it, dear?'

'He doesn't seem too upset about the actual murder,' Rose answered, 'but he can't think of anything else, and the police have been positively badgering him. It was bad enough when Superintendent Tenterden was here alone, but there's a man from Scotland Yard, and – well, I can't help it, Mummy, I just get a feeling that he's terrifying Daddy.'

'But Rose, what do you mean?'

44

'I wish I knew,' Rose said uneasily. 'It's something in the way Daddy talks to him, in the way he looks at him. I can't really make out what he feels about Jensen, either. He didn't know the man very well, did he?'

'He gave him the night-watchman's job because of his injury,' her mother answered. She was a slighter, shorter woman than her daughter, and after nearly thirty years, still a little surprised that she had married one of the Richardsons. The daughter of a local tradesman, she had been Rose's grandfather's secretary, quiet, pretty, and efficient. At the time of the marriage, Sydney had risked his father's anger, and defied threats to throw him out of the firm. Yet in his last years the old man had depended on Sydney's wife.

'I'll try to persuade him to talk tonight, Rose,' she said, 'but he may just shut up if you're in.'

'I'll spend the evening with Lucy,' Rose Richardson said. 'But I don't think he'll tell you anything, Mummy. I think he's buried it in himself.'

7
A LITTLE KNOWLEDGE

AS ROGER and Tenterden walked away from the wages
office towards the gates the girl they had seen a few minutes
before walked past them; and by the time they had reached the
spot where the men were working on the broken bicycle-lamp
glass she passed them at the wheel of a scarlet MG. The engine
snorted, and it was almost as if she were saying how much she
disliked the way the police had talked to her father. Tenterden
was frowning when he said:

'That girl will get into trouble if she drives too fast – things
are a bit feudal round here, Handsome.'

'So I've noticed,' Roger said. 'But what made you say it
this time?'

'She's got one bad habit – of driving at fifty on the
roads leading out of Corby, and sometimes along Factory
Road at weekends. Safe enough, I daresay, but if anyone
else were to do it our chaps would charge 'em. She gets away
with it.'

'Does Richardson get away with anything?'

'I wouldn't like to be sure,' answered Tenterden. 'What
worries me is that if the local coppers will let Rose get away
with speeding, what will they let others get away with?'

What would Tenterden himself wink at, for instance.

'Who are the feudal lords and masters?' asked Roger.

'Only two of them really – Sydney Richardson and Sir
Lancelot Key – he's the senior partner, by about five years in
age and half a million pounds in stock. Richardson's a nephew
on the Richardson side, the Keys are the real big shots,
although Richardson is in control down here. Funny set-up,
really. Sir Lancelot has a son in London, at the London office
most of the time. Young Peter Key isn't a go-getter like
Rose Richardson, he's a stickler for rule and regulation – you
never catch him out doing thirty-five where he ought to be
doing thirty. Old Key's a widower and Mrs Richardson isn't
a feudal type, so really and truly there's Sir Lancelot Key,
Richardson, and Rose who might throw their weight about.

They'd do it as a kind of natural right, you know. Be shocked if they realized they were doing it.'

'No one else but these three?'

'There's Paul, the family black sheep,' Tenterden answered. 'Half-brother to Peter – Sir Lancelot Key's son by his first marriage. He used to be one of the directors, but he's out of the business, and seldom comes near here now. If he did he'd throw his weight about all right. At one time it looked as if he and Rose were going to make a match of it, but Richardson put a stop to it.'

'Why?'

'Dunno,' said Tenterden, 'but I think it was because of this Paul Key's reputation for wine, women, and horse-racing. Anyhow, he's been out of the company for a long time. Richardson and the other Keys bought him out.'

'Bought him out, did they?' remarked Roger, and then changed the subject by asking: 'Any idea why Blake didn't report his wife was missing?'

'I can't believe that Charlie —' Tenterden began, then broke off, without labouring the point that he was too deeply involved with the natives to be wholly detached about any of them. He led the way more briskly towards the spot which had been cordoned off, without answering Roger's question. Here, several uniformed policemen were keeping a crowd of fifty people away from the cordon, and Brown and several detectives were searching the ground. The broken glass had been put on a sheet of paper, and marked *'Believed to be bicycle-lamp glass, found at point marked 9 on diagram'*, and was dated and timed. A youngish man who looked too small to be a policeman or a member of the local Criminal Investigation Department was standing at a small blackboard with a sheet of white paper attached to it, and he had prepared the diagram, with numbered spots showing where the glass, the pump, the tracks, the heel marks, and other things had been found; there were several items new to Roger. A handkerchief had been found in the long grass, a man's heel-print close to the bicycle, the footprints of three men near the spot where a car had been parked the previous night. There were notes, too: the tyres were Dunlop, size 5.50×15, and might have been fitted on any small car. *Little used* was noted in parenthesis against the tyre size.

Brown was in his element.

'No need for me to stay here,' said Roger, and looked farther along towards the silo, where a fire escape was standing, skeleton-like against the sky, with two men on it. A larger crowd of people had gathered there, and Tenterden said:

'I told them to cover the girl up so that no one would know who she was, but the firemen will know, and they'll talk. If you want to see Blake before he knows his wife's body's been found, you'd better be quick.'

'Take me to him, will you?' asked Roger.

Tenterden nodded, and still did not answer the question: why had Blake failed to report that his wife had been missing all night? Instead, he said:

'Blake lives in a cottage he took over forty years ago, nothing could ever persuade him to move. He could afford a much better place, of course, but he hates changes.'

Roger said: 'Oh.'

They drove straight towards Corby, through the town, where everyone paused to stare, to point, and to comment, and to another terrace of small, red-bricked Victorian cottages. At the back, Roger saw, were tiny gardens and a service road. A few people were in the street, Park Terrace, and three small cars and two motor scooters were parked outside cottages. Tenterden pulled up outside Number 17. Roger watched the curtains at the small front window, but nothing seemed to move. Neighbours watched as they reached the front door, and Tenterden rattled the letter-box; there was neither bell nor knocker. Footsteps sounded immediately, and Charlie Blake opened the door.

Tenterden said clearly: 'Charlie, we want a word with you about that guillotine,' so that the nearby people could hear, and after a pause, Blake said:

'Please come in.' There was scarcely room in the small passage for all three men, and Blake opened the door of the front room. The ceiling was so low that Roger ducked. Blake looked exactly as he had at the factory, even against a background of flowered wallpaper, framed photographs, old fashioned saddle-back armchairs, thick lace curtains, and a wide mantelpiece with several small silver cups on it – sporting trophies of some kind.

'What is it you would like to know?' Blake asked.

'Do you service the guillotine regularly?' asked Roger.

'Once every week, without fail.'

48

'When did you last service it?'

'On Tuesday,' answered Blake.

'Was it in perfect condition?'

'Yes, I would say that.'

'What was the cause of the breakdown today?'

'One of the holding bolts worked loose, so the blade wasn't cutting clean,' answered Blake. 'With a machine like that you have to have it exactly right, it's a precision instrument. A thousandth of an inch out can give it the wrong angle for cutting, and once that starts the edges of the book get rough, so the angle error gets greater.' Blake spoke mechanically, as if his mind wasn't really on what he was saying.

'Has that bolt ever worked loose before?' asked Roger.

'I've known it happen.'

'Did you check it yourself?'

'Yes, Mr West, I did,' answered Blake, and he drew himself up. 'That's a very dangerous machine, if it goes wrong. If the guillotine were to fall a second too soon, or if one of the bolts gave way, it could cut a man's fingers off, even cut his hand off. I don't take any chances with the guillotine, and I do everything to it myself. But the bolt *can* work loose. There would be a little too much oil, or some dust, which prevents a proper tightening, that's why Malloy – the guillotine operator – checks it every morning and reports to me if he thinks there's anything wrong. And it has been working very heavily of late. There is a big order going through for urgent delivery, and the machine trims twice as many as the small one.'

'What time was it reported this morning?' asked Roger.

'Just after eight o'clock,' said Blake. He closed his eyes, and hesitated, and then went on: 'I was an hour late at the works this morning, I – I had a restless night. So I didn't see the report until nine o'clock, otherwise I would have put it right sooner. It's my fault that the guillotine was held up for so long.'

'Not often you're late, is it?' asked Tenterden.

'No.'

'Why did you have a bad night, Mr Blake?' asked Roger.

Blake didn't answer.

'Any special reason, Charlie?' Tenterden could not keep in the background for long.

Blake closed his eyes again, and clenched his hands, and there was no doubt that he was a man suffering from some great strain. He moistened his lips, began to speak, stopped, and then said huskily:

'Yes, there was. My wife didn't come home. She wasn't here when I got back from the Rose and Crown last night, and – she stayed away all night.' He broke off, and seemed to be fighting against a breakdown; when he spoke again his voice was almost inaudible. 'I've been afraid that she would leave me,' he said. 'I've been afraid that she would leave me for a younger man.'

Roger glanced at Tenterden sharply. The local man had known about this, of course, and an obvious possibility screeched at him that the other man was the dead night-watchman. That would give Blake the strongest possible motive.

'Who was this man?' Roger demanded.

Blake stared at him blindly.

Then the silence was broken by a car drawing up outside. Both Roger and Tenterden noticed it, but Blake appeared oblivious. Car doors slammed. Roger caught a glimpse of two men getting out of it, and thought they were Tenterden's men. Tenterden seemed reluctant to go and open the door, but went without being prompted. Roger felt resentment welling up against the Corby superintendent. It was one thing to want the Yard to handle the people with whom he was personally involved. It was another to withhold information, even for a few hours.

Blake was standing and looking rather like a church dignitary, tall, lean body rigid, hands still clenched by his side, eyes screwed up.

'Who was the man involved in your fears, Mr Blake?'

'I don't know,' Blake said, whispering. 'I don't know who it was, only that there was another man.' He backed towards a large armchair, and lowered himself slowly. Voices sounded outside, on a low key. 'She used to go to an old school friend of hers every Wednesday and Saturday night. I was happy she had someone to visit, it meant that I could go out as usual, and she wouldn't be at home by herself, but – she didn't just see her friend.'

'How do you know she went out with any man?'

'It was easy to tell,' answered Blake, still huskily. 'It was the way she changed, the way she looked at me, and – there was the smell of tobacco on her clothes. She doesn't smoke and I don't, either, and I'm very sensitive to the odour of tobacco.' He seemed to be talking to himself, as if he was glad to be able to give voice to these thoughts at last. 'I don't know who it is, but there's another man, and – now she's left me:'

Tenterden called: 'Can you spare a moment, Superintendent?'

Roger thought, I'm going to have trouble with you, that's sticking out a mile, and called back: 'In a minute.' He looked bleakly into Blake's eyes and saw the pain in them and did not know the real cause of that pain. He had to find out quickly. There were influences at work here which he didn't like at all. If Tenterden was soft-pedalling, he, Roger, had to go all out. And Blake was in a corner, and might even be the killer; the pressure must be remorseless. 'Blake, what is the name of the man your wife is going with?'

'I don't know!'

'I believe you do.'

'I tell you I don't know the name of the man! I don't even want to know it, if I knew who it was I would — '

Blake caught his breath. His hands were unclenched now and stretched out in front of him, the fingers crooked, and there was an expression of hatred on his face. His teeth were actually bared. He checked his words, but could not check his manner, or his trembling, or the way his fingers were crooked.

Then, he said: 'I love her! I love her so much the fear of losing her is driving me out of my mind.' He closed his eyes again, and Roger heard a creak at the door, guessed that Tenterden was just outside. If Tenterden broke this up, Roger would tear a strip off him. The door didn't open any wider. 'I didn't think such a thing could happen to me, I didn't think that a young and beautiful woman could ever marry me. When she did, I was the happiest man in Corby, the happiest man alive. And then I realized that she was going with this other man.'

He stopped.

'Why don't you name this man?' demanded Roger harshly.

There was a flash of anger in Blake's eyes.

'Are you calling me a liar, Superintendent?'

'I think you know the man.'

'And I tell you that I have no idea who he is,' answered Blake. 'And if I had, what business is it of yours? If my wife chooses to leave me, it has nothing to do with the police.'

51

'Provided nothing happens to the man, it's not.'

Blake began: 'What —?' And then the anger faded. It was impossible to be sure whether his new expression showed simply alarm, or astonishment, or sudden fear, or simply the surprise of realizing what these questions were leading up to '*Do you mean* —' he began in a squeaky voice, but the words faltered in mid-air.

'What is the name of the man your wife was seeing?' demanded Roger.

'As God is my judge,' said Blake, in a slow, deliberate voice, 'I don't know the man's name.' He paused, stood up from the arm of the chair, and asked, 'Do you know, Superintendent?'

This was Tenterden's cue, and he took it. The door opened wider, and he came into the room, massive and comfortable looking, as if oblivious of the fact that he might be choosing the wrong moment. But he had taken the pressure off Blake smoothly and cleverly.

'Can you spare me a minute, Mr West?'

'I'll be with you in a moment,' Roger said roughly, and glowered. The local man hesitated, then flushed a little and backed out of the room. He closed the door. Blake was staring at Roger, but his eyes had a glazed look, as if he were aware only of pain. 'Blake,' Roger said, 'it might be of extreme importance for us to know the name of the man with whom you believe your wife associates. The only wise thing is to tell the truth. Do you understand?'

Blake muttered: 'Yes.'

'What is the man's name?'

'I don't know,' said Blake. 'I didn't dare try to find out, for fear of what I might do to him.'

Blake didn't say anything more, and it was impossible to be sure whether he was lying to save himself or whether he was telling the truth. There wasn't any doubt that Tenterden had interrupted deliberately, but this wasn't the moment to have it out with him. Roger went out, nodded to the Corby man as they went outside the cottage. A crowd had gathered, thirty or forty people, mostly youngsters. A man was saying:

'Now get off, you kids, there's no need for you to hang around here.'

'What's new?' Roger asked in a low-pitched voice.

'It was Doris Blake all right.'

52

'How was she killed?'

'Manual strangulation, that's certain now.'

'Where is she?'

'We've got a cellar at the station which we use as a morgue.'

'What about a pathologist?'

'Dr Owen was coming over tonight from Colchester anyhow, with a full report on Jensen, so he can do the autopsy. The local police surgeon, Dr Arnold, will help.'

'When will the woman be at the morgue and fairly presentable?' Roger was still brusque.

'You mean, for an identification?'

'Yes.'

'Give them half an hour.'

'All right,' said Roger. He saw that not only the youngsters in the crowd but also the adults who had joined them and the local police were watching him and Tenterden, as if trying to make out what they were saying. From the moment he had arrived there had been a feeling of being watched, and it wasn't going to get any less acute. He had a feeling, too, that in spite of the men coming from Colchester, Corby was isolated. Anything that happened to anyone in Corby was the whole town's business. Anyone in trouble had to be protected by the town. 'Do you know if Doris Blake was having an affair with Jensen?'

Tenterden hesitated, and then said heavily:

'Yes. They were meeting at R. & K.'s twice a week.'

'It's time we had a talk, to clear the air,' Roger said flatly. 'Let's get in the car, where we can't be overheard.' They squeezed in, watched by a crowd which refused to move on. The doors slammed. 'Listen, Arthur,' Roger said, 'you're doing all you can to help Blake. You're keeping facts from me, too. What's this all about?'

Tenterden stared straight ahead at two boys leaning on the front of the car.

'I told you this wasn't my job,' he said.

'Now, easy,' Roger said. 'You haven't handed in your resignation, have you?'

Tenterden answered: 'No, you know I haven't, and I know that means I'm still a copper. All right, I'm a copper. I knew something which pointed to Charlie, and I'm all for Charlie, so I made sure I couldn't let prejudice get in the way.'

'You didn't have to lie to me.'

53

'You discovered it without help from me.'

'Hours late.'

'What do a few hours matter?' demanded Tenterden.

Roger hesitated. Much of his anger had evaporated, he could understand Tenterden's anxiety not to allow his personal knowledge to affect his judgement either way. There was another fact: a few hours couldn't matter much – except that for personal reasons he wanted to be free after three o'clock tomorrow afternoon; he didn't want to waste any time at all. He must watch himself, but he must also watch Tenterden.

He said: 'An hour could make a hell of a lot of difference, and you know it. If we can prove it's Blake, time's unimportant. If it wasn't, we haven't even made a start. So I want to find out one way or the other.'

Tenterden said. 'All right, Handsome. How?'

'I want Blake to identify his wife's body, now.'

Tenterden began: 'Listen, Handsome —'

'We can judge from his reaction whether he knew she was dead or not.'

'But if he doesn't know, it's torture.'

'Like Jensen suffered. Like Doris Blake suffered.'

Tenterden said gruffly: 'Have it your own way.'

'That's the ticket,' Roger said briskly. 'I'll have another go at him. Have a shorthand writer outside the door, will you?'

A quarter of an hour later, Blake was sitting back in a big chair, all his colour gone, perspiration heavy on his forehead, the tension in his body almost intolerable. Roger had questioned him solidly and steadily, not once raising his voice, simply forcing the same questions over and over again about the guillotine, because he believed that Blake had a guilt complex about that, and also about the identity of his wife's man friend. Blake did not crack; if he was going to, it would be at the sight of his wife's body.

'Blake, I want you to come with us and identify a body,' Roger said brusquely. 'It won't take long.' He watched the man intently, but saw nothing to suggest that Blake realized whose body it would be.

The crowd had increased to at least a hundred people, and Roger realized that the identity of the body in the silo had got around; these people weren't simply curious about the police visit to Blake, they knew why the police were here.

54

There was a hush as two policemen opened the door of Tenterden's car, but before Roger and Blake used it, a small man stepped forward from the crowd, dodged the policemen who were protecting the cordon, and reached Charlie Blake.

'You needn't worry, Charlie,' he said quietly. 'No one believes you did it. We've known you too long for that. You haven't got a thing to worry about.'

Blake said heavily: 'Did what, Will?'

'We all want you to know we blame —' the man named Will began.

'That's enough, sir,' Roger said crisply. 'Move aside, please.' He hustled Blake forward, and Blake did not try to hold back, but bent double so as to get into the back of the car. Roger joined him, Tenterden and another Corby man went into the front. Close to the window there was a sea of young faces, which vanished as the car moved off. It was only five minutes' drive to the police station, where at least forty people were in the street. As they got out, a woman called:

'You'll be all right, Charlie!'

Blake looked bewildered, as if he really didn't know what this was all about. Was he pretending to be too dumb?

The cellar was approached from a passage at the back of the old police-station building. Tenterden led the way down a flight of wooden steps, then into a small, brightly lit room with some green steel filing cabinets round the walls. The floor was of concrete, and the room struck chill.

The body, covered with a white sheet, lay on a trestle table with a marble top, a home-made mortuary slab. No one was on duty down there. Tenterden stood by Blake's side, and Roger went to the trestle table, stood on the side opposite Blake, and then turned back the sheet.

Doris Blake looked as if she were sleeping.

'Do you know —?' Roger began, but didn't finish.

Blake stared at the face of his dead wife for perhaps ten seconds, his lips parted, his hands raised, his breathing hushed. Horror showed in his eyes, and then died out of them as the lids closed, he folded up in a faint.

Tenterden held and then supported him to an upright chair. As he straightened up, the Corby superintendent looked at Roger as if he hated him.

8

NIGHT WORK

'HE NEEDS a doctor,' Tenterden said harshly. 'Even you won't torture him any more.'

'Listen, Arthur,' Roger answered quietly. 'I came down here to do a job at your request. I'm doing it the best way I can. If you're going to hold a brief for Blake, you're going to get in my way. Want that?'

They were alone in the little morgue, where it was so chilly. Tenterden was near the unconscious Blake's chair. Roger was still on the other side of the home-made mortuary slab, with the dead woman's face, still uncovered, restful, and un-damaged. Tenterden had a bull-doggish look about him, and there was a glitter in his eyes. He said as if with an effort:

'I'm not holding any brief for Charlie, but he's not been found guilty yet. If he did it, he's got to pay for it, but what he pays is up to the judge, not you. Just now, he needs a doctor.'

'Who'll give him a sedative so that he can't talk.'

'He needs a sedative,' Tenterden growled. 'Can't you see he hasn't slept for nights?'

'I can see he's more likely to tell us what he did last night now than after he's had some rest,' Roger retorted, tight-lipped.

'I tell you —'

'Let's have the lot,' Roger interrupted icily. 'Who else are you going to protect? Who else gets special treatment in this feudal area? The Richardsons? The Keys? And what about those I've never heard of yet?'

Tenterden drew in a deep breath.

Roger said: 'When Blake comes round I'm going to question him. Do you intend to be present?'

'No,' Tenterden said hoarsely. 'No, I don't.' He stared at Roger with his eyes still glittering, but his full lips parted; he was breathing very hard. Without another word, he swung round and went out. The door closed slowly behind him, with a sighing squeak.

Roger looked at it, still tight-lipped, then down at Blake,

who hadn't stirred. He looked pale and so very, very tired. 'If he did it, he's got to pay for it, but what he pays is up to the judge,' Tenterden had said, and there were times when Roger would have said exactly the same. Was he going too far? Was this remorseless pressure on Blake really justified? Was he really out to get a record quick finish, so that he could get off to Bedford?

'If he did it, we've got to know now,' Roger said, *sotto voce*. Blake stirred.

Roger gave him two or three minutes, and then asked:

'How long had you known about your wife and Jensen, Blake?'

Blake looked at him with agony in his eyes, and then his face began to pucker up, and he began to cry.

Roger went to the door, opened it, and saw Tenterden and a police sergeant were near by.

'Better get him upstairs and send for a doctor,' he said brusquely. 'There's nothing more I can do now.'

Tenterden said. 'Dr Arnold's on his way.'

Once Arnold had arrived, of course, he would have come into the morgue. Tenterden had declared war over Charlie Blake.

Two questions nagged at Roger.

Was he being too tough?

Or was Tenterden really prepared to protect others in this feudal part of the land?

Dr Arnold was a short, slight, brisk, outwardly officious man, with very black hair and a startlingly white centre parting. He appeared to be completely objective. Blake needed a sedative after the shock. He could not stay alone in his cottage, so the best place was a private ward at the local cottage hospital. There would be facilities for the police to sit by his bedside. Roger made no demur about any of this, Tenterden made no comment, and Blake was taken off in an ambulance, watched by a crowd now much larger; Roger recognized several of the people who had been at the cottage. The ambulance had hardly driven off before a massive Rolls-Royce, of early pre-war vintage, pulled up outside the police station, and a tall, youthful-looking man in purply grey Harris tweeds stepped out, a pink woollen scarf round his neck, a deerstalker hat pulled down on his head. He stood for a moment surveying the crowd, and gave Roger the impression that he rather relished an audience.

'Dr Owen,' Tenterden whispered. It was the first time he had volunteered even a word since stalking out of the morgue.

'Hallo, there,' Dr Owen greeted bluffly. But for his greying hair and the lines at his cheeks and mouth he would have passed for thirty; he was probably fifty-two or three. 'You've got another corpus for me, I understand.' He looked at Roger, and quite suddenly beamed and shot out his hand. 'You're Handsome West,' he declared. 'I saw you giving evidence at the Old Bailey once, and was glad I wasn't in the dock.' He thrust out a big hand, and Roger gripped it. 'Made any arrests yet?'

'Several are pending,' said Roger mildly.

'Glad to hear it.' They turned and walked up the steps of the police station, and Tenterden gave a short but comprehensive report. Owen made little comment, but went with them to the emergency morgue, made what appeared to be a cursory examination of the dead woman, from the waist upwards, and then said: 'I've brought all I need. Going to turn this place into the laboratory again?'

'I think we'd better.'

'Well, get your chaps to bring down my stuff, will you?' asked Owen. 'It's all in the boot, just bring everything.' He handed over a bunch of keys. 'Use the small key with the rusty top. And warn Mr West what a testy individual I am if anyone is breathing down my neck when I'm doing a job like this, won't you?'

'I've met police-surgeon pathologists before,' Roger said, 'and we've got enough on hand to keep us up half the night without crowding you.' Then he made his gesture, turning to Tenterden and saying: 'Arthur, we ought to go and see what's turned up near the works. All right with you?'

'Good idea,' Tenterden said, and looked straight into Roger's eyes as he went on: 'Then we'd better eat. My wife's expecting you and Brown to dinner. Hope you'll come.'

'Be glad to,' Roger said.

So the breach was repaired, temporarily at least.

The situation outside the works hadn't really changed, although new arc lights had been rigged up, there was a vivid

58

concentration of white light around the spot where the car had been parked. A dozen more dots indicated places where articles had been found – including an old pipe, a rusty bicycle wheel which must have been under the hedge for months, cigarette cartons, a half-crown and a sixpence, an old table-knife with a burned handle, and a child's shoe. These were all placed on pieces of brown paper, labelled, and fully described. Brown was looking tired. The young man on the diagram seemed eager to keep at it. Six men were searching farther away from the spot, and another team was working near the silo. Roger and Tenterden drove over to it, and as they drew up, Tenterden said:

'We ought to be able to check if Blake's footprints were at both places. If they weren't it'll be in his favour.'

'He could have worn overshoes,' Roger said, and grinned. 'The biggest thing in his favour might be finding out about the other men – the men from the car. No doubt that his wife's shoes made the heel marks by the hedge, so she came along the road on her bicycle, and then crossed to the other side of the hedge, and walked along wheeling the bicycle. There's no trace of the machine yet, and there isn't likely to be until morning. What we don't know is whether she was attacked by one man or by three. And we don't know whether one man or three broke into the works.'

'Never likely to find out from the clues here,' said Tenterden. 'You serious about having everyone's finger-prints taken?'

'We can stall on that,' Roger said.

'Getting hungry?' asked Tenterden slyly.

'Famished – and I'll bet Browny is.'

Brown said heartily: 'Believe me I am.'

'If we're going to give your wife catering problems —' Roger began.

'She's used to big eaters,' Tenterden said, and drove them to a small Georgian house, painted white and black, and looking beautiful in a terrace of houses all two hundred years or more old.

Margaret Tenterden was a tall, slim woman, so expertly made-up that she seemed almost out of place in Corby. Her auburn hair was dressed in a fashion from *Vogue,* her skin had an artificially natural look, her eyes had a touch of eyeshadow, to heighten their deep and startling blueness, and she was wearing a sheath-like dress which would have done

Knightsbridge and Mayfair justice. On the surface there was nothing amiss between Roger and Tenterden, and nothing spoiled a meal of roast beef and Yorkshire pudding, with fruit salad and cream for dessert.

'Now you can all go and puff smoke in the front room,' she said. 'Maude will help me wash up in the morning, Arthur. Then I'm going along to the Fête meeting – goodness knows what time I'll be back.'

In an L-shaped front room Tenterden produced fat cigars and a good brandy. Brown looked a little out of his depth, and Roger noted with appreciation how beautifully appointed and beautifully kept the room was. There was a Parker Knoll suite, of wine red and gold, a faintly patterned wine-red carpet, gold-coloured curtains with deep pelmets against white-painted woodwork, small pieces of French and English Regency furniture. This not only spelt taste, it spelt money. And if he cared to see it that way, he was being softened up.

The need now was to get rid of Brown, then have things out with Tenterden.

The telephone bell rang near Tenterden, and he lifted the receiver.

'Yes, speaking,' he said. 'Yes.' He glanced at Roger and mouthed something which Roger didn't catch. Then his expression changed, he reminded Roger vividly of his anger in the morgue – even the glitter was back in his eyes.

'Hold on,' he said, then stood up clumsily, stared down at Roger, and said: 'Blake tried to kill himself. Jumped from a window at the hospital. Catching his clothes on a post saved him.'

Tenterden stopped, but his eyes and his manner seemed to accuse:

'That's how far you goaded him.'

Brown demanded urgently: 'Is he hurt much?'
'No,' said Tenterden.
'Looks as if he did the murders all right.'
Tenterden said: 'I always thought you chaps—' and broke off.

Brown looked bewildered.
Roger said: 'Is there anything else, Arthur?'
'What else do you expect?'
'I'd like to know if the missing bicycle's been found, and if

60

Blake's footprints were found near the tyre prints and the bicycle,' Roger said. 'Browny, get over to the station, check on those two things and let me know the result, and check on Blake's condition.'

Brown stood up almost with alacrity.

'Right,' he said.

'Glad I brought someone who'll sacrifice comfort to duty,' Roger said.

Tenterden saw Brown to the front door, while Roger sipped his brandy, drew hard at his cigar, and found himself wondering where the money came from here – it certainly didn't come from Tenterden's salary, which wasn't likely to be more than fifteen hundred a year. Had his wife money? He had to remember that one of the major influences on the investigation would be the local tradition, influences, and prejudices.

Tenterden came back, as Roger stood up. They faced each other, as if sparring for an opening.

Roger said: 'You think I drove Blake to try to kill himself, Arthur; I think his wife did. If you'd wanted to protect anybody you wouldn't have sent to the Yard so quickly, that makes me a bloody fool for asking who else you're protecting. Right?'

Tenterden's big body seemed to relax.

'Right,' he said. 'Handsome words by Handsome West. Truth is, I think more of Charlie than any man I know. Always have. It dates back to school days. He once pulled me out of a flooded river.' The Corby man paused, then went on deliberately: 'This doesn't mean I don't think you were too tough on him, but you only set it off – Doris was his trouble. Whether he killed her or not, it's going to be a big problem. Want all the background now?'

'Please.'

'Doris Blake was on the shelf when Charlie married her,' Tenterden went on, as if really anxious to talk. 'He'd been in love with her for years but hadn't told anyone but a few of his close friends, including me. He and his first wife got along all right, but between you and me she had a hell of a temper – drank a bit in secret, too. Charlie took it as it came. He didn't breathe a word to Doris Miller, as she was then. She worked on one of the binding machines, she'd been at the works since she left school – that's fifteen years. It's an old machine, always wanting a lot of engineering maintenance. That's how they got

61

to know each other, but according to my information, when Charlie popped the question a year after his first wife died, Doris was flabbergasted. She said yes pretty quick, though.

'I never asked any questions, but I think Charlie treated her as if she was made of precious china,' Tenterden went on. 'Afraid to touch her – bit afraid that if he overdid bed life it would upset her. About three months ago, she started going to see Jensen at the works at night, instead of spending the evening with a friend. Two of our chaps reported it to me, and I had a word with Sydney Richardson. If he'd wanted it stopped, I'd have stopped it.'

'So that's why he was so shaken when he knew that Doris Blake was killed too,' Roger remarked.

'That's it,' agreed Tenterden. 'Take it from me, he assumes that Charlie had a brainstorm.'

'It's still possible,' Roger said mildly. 'Brief me about the other people concerned – for instance, Sydney Richardson and the other works bosses, will you? If Richardson didn't mind Jensen and one of the employees having an *affaire* at the works by night it suggests a queer attitude on his part, doesn't it?' When Tenterden didn't answer, Roger went on: 'And Blake's an old employee, almost a friend. Why should Richardson give tacit approval to Blake's wife and Jensen using the works as a love nest?'

'Not much you miss, Handsome, I must say,' Tenterden said ruefully. 'I don't know, for certain. Sydney Richardson's a bit unpredictable, very nervous type, and he makes a fetish of public relations with the workers. As a matter of fact, he's never been quite the same since the big strike, a year or two back. He always believed that the manager-relationship here was so good that his people would defy the unions, but they didn't. Since then he's been edgy, trying to make sure that such a thing couldn't happen again. There have been times when I've wondered whether Sydney R.'s lost his mental balance. Sometimes he behaves as if he's a bit potty.'

It would have been easy to say that this was obviously the heart of the matter; saying so wouldn't help. Roger made himself speak briskly.

'I get it. There was a big strike, and Richardson was naïve enough to make himself believe that the workers here would defy their union, but they didn't. Who led them out? If he's gone mad, whom would he hate? Whom does he blame for the trouble?' When Tenterden didn't answer, Roger asked sharply: 'Did Charlie Blake have anything to do with the strike? Was he against the management?'

After a long pause, Tenterden said: 'In a way, you could say he was. He was the one man who might have swayed the works, but he didn't try. Richardson and Sir Lancelot Key himself tried to make him, but he said it wasn't an issue for him or his union – he's an engineer – and he wouldn't interfere. Wouldn't have made any difference if he had, but he didn't even try. That upset Richardson and Key pretty badly. It may be why Richardson didn't put a stop to Jensen having a visitor when he was on duty at night.'

Before Roger could comment, the telephone bell rang again. Tenterden answered it, then said. 'Hold on,' and held out the receiver. 'It's Brown,' he said.

Roger said into the mouthpiece: 'Yes, Browny?'

Browny said: 'They've found the bicycle under some loose hay near the silo, Handsome, and they've got a footprint from Charlie Blake near the broken glass – the glass was on top of it, so it's not conclusive, but he could have hidden the bike all right.'

Roger said: 'Yes. Anything else?'

'Owen and Arnold have finished their jobs,' Brown said. 'You ought to come and have a talk to them.'

'Right away,' said Roger.

He told Tenterden, who made no comment, but said heavily: 'We'd better be going, hadn't we?'

Doris Blake had died from manual strangulation; there was no contributory cause of death. Scratches on her shoes and bruises on her arms suggested that she had struggled, and had been dragged along the ground.

Jensen had died from cerebral haemorrhage caused by at least four blows on the back of the head by a hammer or similar instrument.

The only finger-prints on Doris Blake's bicycle were her own and her husband's. Two of Blake's footprints were near the spot where the bicycle had fallen.

A check of the tyres of all cars belonging to anyone who worked at the works showed that no such car had been parked near the works gates – that car must have belonged to someone outside the works staff.

Charlie Blake was in a perfect position to make keys for the main gates of the works – one of his jobs was the cutting of keys for general works purposes.

'We want everything checked and rechecked,' Roger said to Tenterden. 'If nothing else turns up by tomorrow midday we'll have to charge Blake.'

'I know,' Tenterden said gruffly. 'I suppose I always did. But that car —'

His voice trailed off.

'I have nothing to say,' said Charlie Blake, in a low-pitched voice, when he was charged, 'except that I know nothing about the murders.'

Roger doubted whether even Tenterden was really convinced, but Brown certainly was. There was no better man to look after the collating of evidence, and Roger's last lingering doubts about going to Bedford were removed when he heard that Richardson was going to London for the weekend.

'Have the Yard keep an eye on him,' Roger said, 'and call me if anything turns up.'

'Such as the men in that car?' Brown was inclined to scoff. 'You're almost as anxious as our Arthur to see Blake in the clear.'

'Don't you believe it,' Roger said. 'I just want a nice clean job. Anything from Pratt and Asterley?'

'Not much,' said Brown, and looked thoughtful. 'One thing would interest us, though, if this was a robbery or hold-up job. Richardson often gives work to old lags. He's a big boy in the local Discharged Prisoners' Aid Society. Pratt recognized a chap named Ragg who was sent down for race-course robberies a few years ago. He and two others, named Carter and Tate, worked the race-courses together. Carter and Tate got off, Ragg got two years.'

'Recognition mutual?' demanded Roger.

'Shouldn't think so. Pratt was in a Division at the time, not at the Yard.'

'Hmm. Have him check all of Richardson's ex-prisoners,' Roger advised, 'but don't raise any scare. See if Tate and Carter are around, too.'

'No need to raise a scare,' Brown said comfortably. 'We've got our man.'

64

9

WILFUL DAMAGE

Driving alone had its drawbacks. The hedges slid by, traffic was thin on the country roads, and the sun wasn't low enough in the west to dazzle. There was time for Roger to think, to let the facts slide through his mind.

Half-way between Corby and Bedford, he was uneasy and even depressed. How right was Tenterden? How right had he himself been? If Blake had broken down into a confession it would have been sufficient justification, but all they had was a broken man and circumstantial evidence – and this news from the two Yard men at the works. One worker once convicted of robbery with violence was at Richardson and Key's – and there might be others, for Richardson the jumpy and the nervous, the man who might have an unreasoning grudge against Blake, made a habit of employing old lags. Well, a lot of good men did that – as often as not it paid off. Now – well, there was the evidence of three men in a car near the gates, wasn't there? Take that away and no one would have much doubt about Blake's guilt.

Roger was on the outskirts of Bedford when he decided to call Brown, drove to police headquarters, received a warm if startled welcome, and at a quarter to seven was talking to Brown, who was still in his office at the Corby station.

'Now what's on your mind?' demanded Brown.

'Man named Ragg,' Roger said.

'And one named Tate, a third named Carter – all old lags, from the north-east,' Brown retorted drily. 'What about them?'

'Check if one of them has a car with tyres size 5.50×15,' Roger said, 'and check their footprints. If they were by those gates we want a lot of questions answered.'

'Still want to soft pedal this angle?'

'Yes,' Roger said.

He reached his brother-in-law's home a little after seven o'clock, and as he pulled up outside, the door opened and his two sons, Martin called Scoopy and Richard called Richard, came hurrying out, delighted. For the first time, he forgot Corby. Janet was in the kitchen with her sister, and both were talking animatedly to a brother they had not seen for five years, and to his wife, a small, smiling, friendly woman from Kentucky. Twenty-seven relatives made the atmosphere of family union complete and boisterously happy. Thoughts of Blake, of his dead wife, of Jensen with his head smashed in, became shadowy things at the back of Roger's mind. He wished he had done the finger-printing, though. It might have been superfluous, but it could also have established if an unauthorized person had been in that wages office on the night of Jensen's murder. He was thinking of this when he was undressing in the small room allocated to him and Janet, at nearly one o'clock that morning. The bed was little more than a large single one, pushed into a corner. Janet sat up on the pillows, watched him, and, quite out of the blue, asked:

'What's worrying you, Roger?'

'Who's worrying?' Roger demanded.

'You know very well what I mean,' Janet said. 'Aren't you satisfied that Blake's the murderer? I heard about him being charged on the radio.'

'Reason says he's the boy,' answered Roger with forced brightness. 'I should really have laid on a big-scale finger-printing job, but it would have taken a couple of days. I couldn't have laid it on and then left it to the others, so I suppose the real truth is I told myself it would be a waste of time, and came here.'

'Old Man Conscience after you again,' Janet said lightly. 'Is it too late to lay it on now?'

'Yes.'

'It's about the first time in ten years you put off a police job for me,' said Janet practically. 'If you hadn't managed to get here I'd have been on your conscience all right!'

Roger forced a laugh, and slid into bed.

Janet dropped off to sleep first, but Roger lay awake for some time. Janet was right from her point of view, but how wrong had he been? How much too eager to believe in Blake's guilt? He kept picturing Blake throwing himself out of that window.

In the next room the brother-in-law from Kentucky was snoring loudly. Downstairs, on a bed made up on the floor, the boys were sound asleep. A hundred miles away, in the remand cell, Blake would be restless. Not so far from Blake, Tenterden was in the twin bed next to his unexpectedly attractive wife. Matter-of-fact Brown was probably fully satisfied that there was nothing to worry about; he would be snoring. But if they had charged the wrong man the killer or killers were still at large. And if that was so, then Roger hadn't any idea even about the motive for the crimes.

He slept soundly once he did get off, but telephoned Brown first thing next morning. Blake seemed to be resigned to his situation, Brown said, and nothing else had turned up.

'You let yourself go, Skipper,' Brown advised. 'All there is to do here is tidy up the odds and ends. Why, even our Arthur's beginning to admit the worst.'

'Make sure the ends are really tied up,' Roger urged. 'Anything new about Richardson's discharged prisoners?'

'Only one there could be any doubt about is Ragg,' Brown told him. 'The others are married, settled down, and have alibis for the Jensen murder. Ragg's got a kind of alibi, too – he was playing darts at a pub in Corby.'

'Does he own a car?'

'No,' said Brown, as if that settled that.

When he rang off, Roger saw that massive Martin called Scoopy was in the room, watching him, and tall Richard called Richard was just outside, saying:

'Come on, Scoop.'

'Worried about this job, Dad?' asked Scoop.

Roger said: 'I am a bit, old chap, but you go and do whatever you're planning to do.'

Martin hesitated, but soon went off.

Had he been at home, Roger would have been preoccupied all the time, but the high spirits of everyone else infected him. He went to bed late that night, and slept soundly until after nine. A telephone call at ten o'clock brought Richard springing up the stairs, calling:

'For you, Dad. The Yard.'

Roger couldn't get downstairs quickly enough, taking it for granted that this was something to do with Corby, even though it didn't come from there.

It was Hardy, working on Sunday like so many of his men.

'Sorry to worry you this morning,' the Assistant Commissioner said, 'but Brown tells me everything's over at Corby bar the shouting.'

'Looks like it,' Roger said.

'Good. Then come back here tomorrow, will you? And think over the Sparkham job today. There's some talk of a defence alibi – we don't want a slip up over that.'

'My God we don't!' Roger exclaimed.

He drove the family back to London early on Monday, and went straight to the Yard. The Sparkham case was in a state of confusion, chiefly because a Divisional man had unearthed what seemed to be an alibi. Roger spent Monday checking.

There was no change at Corby, where Brown said tidying-up was nearly done. Ragg's alibi for the night of the murder had a weakness – he could have been away from the pub for an hour – but perfect alibis were as often suspect.

It was at half past ten on Tuesday when Brown came on the line. His voice told of trouble, and Roger's heart began to pound. Had Blake tried suicide again, and succeeded? Surely he would be too closely watched.

'Don't know whether it's anything to do with our job or not,' said Brown. 'Very peculiar thing's happened down here, Skipper.'

'What is it?'

'You remember the Composing Room?'

'Of course I do.' Brown could be prosy when he was worried. 'You know that as the operators work on the type-setting machines, the Monotypes, they punch little holes in spools, which are sent downstairs to have the wording cast in metal.'

'I know how it works,' Roger said, and stifled his impatience.

'Well, they don't always go straight to the machines,' Brown went on. 'They're marked and indexed, then stored – sometimes for two or three days, sometimes for a week or two. This lot's been there for ten days, put aside for another edition of the big text-book order they gas about. The casters often fall behind the keyboards, too – the spools are kept in readiness for weeks at a time.'

'Well?'

'Well, a whole box of these things, about sixty of them in all, have been found destroyed,' said Brown. 'There may be more. Someone has been at them with a hammer and acid. Made a proper mess. The thing is, they were in that box last Wednesday, so the damage could have been done same time as the murders.'

'Any sign of blood anywhere?' Roger demanded. 'Any

68

indication that the hammer used to kill Jensen was used on those spools?'

'There are some marks, and they're almost certainly blood,' Brown told him. 'I've had some of the spools sent to Dr Arnold here for analysis, but he's out on his morning's round, and it might be a couple of hours before he's back. Could get the job done at a hospital by a junior, but you know what a stickler Arnold is for red tape. I thought you'd better know right away, though.'

'Quite right,' said Roger gruffly. 'I've got a hell of a day here, but I'll come up/first thing in the morning. You keep me posted. Any news about the three old lags and that car?'

'Can't trace any car with 5.50 × 15 size tyres to any of 'em,' answered Brown. 'I'm not satisfied with Ragg's alibi, but I can't really break it.'

'Keep trying,' said Roger. 'Anything else?'

'Well, there is rather a queer development,' said Brown. 'You remember Sydney Richardson's daughter, Rose?'

What the hell was the matter with Brown this morning?

'Yes.'

'She's been going round asking a hell of a lot of questions, and had a blazing row with her father,' Brown said. 'I dunno what it was about.'

'Try to find out,' urged Roger.

He stepped up the pressure on the Sparkham case, interviewed nine witnesses, and established that Sparkham's alibi was phoney; at least that case was going well. It was midnight before he was home, though, and he was anxious to be off at crack of dawn.

In a strange way, he was glad about the Corby development, for it would make sure that he cleared up any lingering doubts. This time he would stay at Corby for a month, if needs be, rather than leave anything to Brown and Tenterden. He had an odd feeling which made no sense; he was glad that Charlie Blake was going to have another chance.

Yet Blake was in a better position than most to sabotage those spools – and if he knew that Richardson had tolerated his wife's *affaire* with Jensen, then he might hate the managing director, and so the firm.

10

ROSE

ROSE RICHARDSON heard about the discovery of the smashed spools just before lunch-time, when she came in from visiting three members of the works staff who were ill. Her father's chair was empty, his desk littered with papers, and his secretary, a young and rather precocious girl with astonishingly long legs and as flat-breasted as a boy, said there was some trouble in the Composing Room.

'Looked as if he'd drop down dead, Miss Rose, and it's no use saying he didn't.'

'All right, Peggy,' said Rose. She hurried out of the wages office and along to the Monotype Room; only a few of the machines were working, most of the men were talking, and there was an awkward pause when Rose went in. The foreman of the department covered it by coming across from his small office, rather like Blake's in the Engineering Shop, and saying:

'Have you heard about the trouble, Miss Rose?'

'Yes. I thought my father was up here.'

'He's gone downstairs to the casters,' the foreman said. 'That's where the damage was done.' As Rose turned to go, he went on a little awkwardly: 'Can you spare me a moment, Miss Rose?'

Most of the operators were tapping the keys of their boards. Rose went into the little office, and the foreman pushed his hand through his hair, still awkwardly, and went on:

'You might say that it's none of my business, but your father seems terribly worried these days, and – well, Miss Rose, when he heard about this I thought he would faint.'

Rose said: 'Have you any idea what's worrying him, Mr Ward?'

'No, I can't say I have. Of course he's always been the worrying kind, but it wasn't until after the strike that he really seemed to be *ill* with it. I know it's none of my business, but we older workers are all very fond of Mr Sydney, we don't like to see him worried.'

'I know,' Rose said, and forced a smile. 'And the younger

workers don't like the way he jumps down their throats. I'm hoping things will soon right themselves.' She turned away and hurried across the shop, with the *tap-tap-tap-tap* of the Monotype keyboards like a refrain. Then she opened the door leading into the Casting Room, and was sharply aware of the acrid smell of molten metal. None of the machines was working. The operatives were standing in a group, and her father was saying in a shrill, squeaky voice:

'One of you must know who did it. You must know!' His eyes were glittering, and the right eye was twitching; she had never seen him look so bad. His hands were clenched and raised, as if he wanted to strike out at one of the men.

None of them spoke.

'It's no use standing there like a lot of dummies!' Richardson shrilled. 'Who did this? Look – who destroyed a week's work by our operators? *Who was it?*'

He flung out his right arm and pointed a quivering finger at some high cupboards, fastened to the walls. Inside were dozens of cartons of the spools which had been punched – rather like the music of a mechanical piano player – ready for the casting. Three of these cartons had been emptied, and the smashed spools littered the floor. It looked as if someone had been let loose with a hammer, almost as if someone had gone beserk and trampled on them savagely, then poured acid over them.

Reed, foreman of the Casting Room, was a short, grey-haired man with a very red face and beady eyes. Rose saw him glance at the men. Several of them were looking angry, most of them were obviously ill-at-ease.

'*I want to know* —' Richardson began.

'Daddy, Uncle Lance is on the telephone. He wants a word with you urgently,' Rose interrupted, pushing past the machines towards her father. 'Do you know how many spools are damaged yet?'

Her father stared at her blankly.

The foreman said: 'So far we've found a hundred and twenty that are no use at all, Miss Rose. There may be more.'

'Have you sent – sent for the police?'

'Yes, Mr Tenterden's on his way.'

'That's good,' said Rose jerkily. She put a hand on her father's arm, and he allowed her to lead him away from the Casting Room into the open air of the yards. His eyes were still glittering, and there was a beading of sweat on his forehead.

She had never seen his face so pale. Not far away was an alley leading to one of the side gates of the works grounds, used by a few people who lived on that side of the works. As she led the way to this, her father didn't speak, even to ask her about the call from his senior partner.

'Daddy,' Rose said quite calmly, 'if you keep behaving like that you'll have much more trouble with the workers. You realize that, don't you?'

She doubted whether he understood what she said. His eyes had a burning glow in them, as if he had terrible headache.

'They simply won't stand for being shouted at,' Rose went on, 'and you can't blame them. They won't make excuses because you're ill, either.'

Her father moistened his lips, and said: 'Who's ill? What's this about being ill?'

'You're ill, and we all know it,' Rose said, in the same matter-of-fact way. 'I didn't realize how much you've been overworking, but you need a long rest.'

'*I'm* not ill!'

'You are, you know,' said Rose. She did not know that she sounded much more adult than her own mother, and as if she were talking to a person much younger than herself. 'I think you have been for a long time. Is there anything worrying you, apart from that?'

'Apart from what?'

'Apart from overwork?'

'I'm not overworked. I'm not ill. I won't have you talking to me like this,' Richardson said jerkily. 'What does Lance want? What's this about a telephone call?'

'There isn't one,' Rose said quietly. 'If I hadn't got you away there would have been an open quarrel between you and the men, and that's the last thing you want.'

'*I* will handle the men,' her father retorted harshly. 'I have been handling them successfully for the past fifteen years, and I don't want teaching by you or by anyone else. Don't interfere with me again, Rose.'

'I won't interfere unless I have to,' Rose said patiently. 'I wish you'd go home and take it easy for the rest of the day. You'd feel better then.'

'Take it *easy*!' cried Richardson. 'Good God, girl, have you gone mad? How can I take it easy at a time like this. That was deliberate sabotage. A whole week's work thrown away.

We have customers pressing for delivery, publishers desperately anxious to get books out, the Machine Room's waiting for work, and you talk about taking things *easy*! You haven't the faintest idea of what you're talking about. Why don't you stop playing at working, and go home and help your mother. Take it *easy*! Why —!'

He choked.

He closed his eyes, and it looked for a moment as if he would faint, but as Rose took his arm, he opened his eyes again, and appeared to recover. Something of the glitter went out of his eyes, he said: 'I'm sorry, Rose,' in a low-pitched voice, and turned and hurried away. He did not go through the Casting Room, but out towards the main gates, then into the main doorway. Rose did not go immediately to his office, but went by the roundabout way to her own. As she did so, she saw Tenterden and the big, heavy man from Scotland Yard, named Brown. Tenterden raised a hand, while Brown gave a formal:

'Good morning, miss.'

'Sorry to hear that there's more trouble,' Tenterden said. 'Not serious, I hope.'

'It is extremely serious,' Rose said coldly. 'For one thing, it seems to be driving my father mad.'

'Upset again, is he?' asked Tenterden.

'Very.'

'Exactly what do you mean, miss, by saying that it's driving your father mad?' asked Brown.

'Production is being held up all the time, and this is a serious loss,' Rose said. 'And nothing like this has ever happened at the works before. This wasn't done by Charlie Blake, either.'

'What makes you say that?' asked Brown owlishly.

She thought, furious with herself, 'I'm as bad as Daddy.' After a pause, she said: 'It's simply that Mr Blake was blamed for the murders, and for the delay on the guillotine, and – well, quite honestly, I'm too upset to know what I'm saying.'

'I quite understand, Miss Rose,' Tenterden said.

Brown grunted, and walked with Tenterden into the offices. Rose stood watching, saw the door swing to behind them, and stayed there for a few moments in vexation. As she waited a van swung into the gates, much too fast, and she had to step quickly out of the way. A man at the gate shouted at the

73

driver, whom Rose recognized as young Tom Cousins; for a moment Cousins looked scared. The incident jolted her mind off her chief anxiety. Cousins, who was in his early twenties, jammed on the brakes, flung open the door, and jumped down.

'I'm ever so sorry, miss, I hope I didn't scare you.'

'If you drive that van like that again I'll recommend that you be taken off driving,' Rose said sharply.

The youth started to retort, stopped himself, muttered 'sorry' again, and went back to the van. As it crawled towards one of the loading bays, Rose found herself smiling. The man who had shouted, the gatekeeper named Gordon, came up to her.

'That's the way to deal with Tom Cousins,' he declared. 'Threaten to take him off driving, and he'll be scared stiff. He loves sitting at the wheel.'

'So do I, but I don't go about nearly breaking people's necks.'

Gordon said mildly: 'We all drive a bit foolish at times, I suppose.'

Rose looked at him, saw the way his rosebud-shaped lips curved, and the twinkle in his light-brown eyes. He had a round, plump face, a little like a turnip, and a crop of almost white hair which looked like down. She laughed.

'I suppose I do speed a bit,' she admitted. 'I'll have to watch myself. Mr Gordon, have you any idea what's worrying my father?'

Gordon's twinkle died away.

'No, Miss Rose,' he answered, 'I only know that something is very heavy on his mind. In the last few weeks he's lost pounds, and — ' He broke off. 'It really began with the strike, didn't it?'

'Are you really sure it began with the strike?'

'Well, it wasn't until afterwards that people began to talk.' There was an apologetic look in Gordon's eyes as he went on: 'You know how it is in Corby, Miss Rose. Everybody talks about everybody else, and the works is no exception. It was common talk just after the strike was settled and everyone came back that Mr Sydney wasn't the same man. It wasn't that he was difficult, or that he tried any reprisals; as a matter of fact, he leaned over backwards to implement the terms of the settlement – no victimization, especially. He tried to pretend that he felt just the same as always, but that's the point, Miss Rose – he tried to look as if nothing had changed, but something had, inwardly.'

'I know exactly what you mean,' Rose said. 'And you feel sure it was the strike?'

'Well, I know that some of us who weren't concerned with the striking unions upset him rather badly,' Gordon said very quietly. 'I did, for one. As gatekeeper I'm not involved in any of the unions concerned, and Mr Sydney wanted me to use my influence with the men to defy the unions, but that kind of thing is too delicate for a man like me to interfere with. It was the same with several others.'

'Including Charlie Blake?'

The small eyes were very steady.

'Yes, Charlie upset Mr Sydney because he wouldn't use his influence against the strike, Miss. Mr Sydney didn't seem to understand that if we did anything, or even tried to, we might have made the situation worse. Things have been all right on the surface since, but underneath – well, I always had a feeling that your father still resented what we'd done. Or rather, what we hadn't done.'

'I see, Mr Gordon,' Rose said, and after a pause she went on: 'I can't believe that the strike would have upset him like that – not for so long, anyhow. And I'm quite sure that he wouldn't hold a grievance against anyone, especially people like you and Charlie Blake. I'm wondering if there might be some other reason for the change in him. Will you see if you can find anything out from the works?' she asked, and added almost hopelessly: 'Someone must have an idea what it is.'

'I can certainly try,' said Gordon, and then he put a hand on Rose's arm. 'Will you forgive me if I speak frankly, Miss Rose?'

'I want you to.'

'You'd get far better results if you asked the shop managers, the foremen, and the chargehands yourself. They all trust you. If anyone knows anything he's more likely to tell you than to tell me – be more likely to tell me to mind my own business!'

'You may be right,' said Rose thoughtfully. 'I'll make some inquiries – both about my father and the damage to the spools.' She looked towards the window of her father's office, and went on: 'I hope nothing else goes wrong. He won't be able to stand it.'

'I shouldn't go looking for trouble,' Gordon advised. 'There's no reason to expect anything else will go wrong, is there?'

'I suppose not, really,' Rose smiled, much more freely. 'Thank you, Mr Gordon, I feel much better for this talk.'

She turned, and went back into the offices.

Rose talked to every departmental manager, every charge-hand and foreman, and to several of the older members of the works staff. Did any of them know anyone with a spite against the company, spite enough to damage all those spools? And had anyone noticed how ill her father looked?

They all said the same: that he had started to look ill about the time of the strike.

11

HOME AFTER DARK

THAT WAS Tuesday.

Every Tuesday, Rose Richardson spent the evening at a Tennis and Social Club, playing a little table tennis, chatting over a drink, and making tentative plans for the club's part in the Corby Summer Fête – an open-air play. This year, after a lot of argument, the committee had decided on *A School for Scandal*. Rose had little enthusiasm for it, nor had Margaret Tenterden, who had been outvoted on the committee, and was always willing to accept a majority vote cheerfully. Rose didn't know her well, liked and admired what she did know of her, but this evening felt a little aloof, chiefly because of Tenterden's activities at the works. She knew that the policeman couldn't help it, and even if he had been difficult it was hardly fair to take it out on his wife, but they exchanged only a word that evening.

Rose couldn't keep her thoughts off her father.

He had come home for dinner, said very little, pleaded a severe headache, and planned to go to bed early. He hadn't said a word to her mother – he seemed never to confide in her. Rose had hesitated about going out, but her mother had told her there was no need to stay in, and she felt a certain relief at having been away from the works and the home atmosphere. But she left early – a little before ten o'clock. As she went out to her car, Margaret Tenterden appeared from the shadows of the car park outside the clubhouse.

Rose started.

'Sorry if I scared you, Rose,' Tenterden's wife said, 'but I wanted a word with you without the others hearing.' She smiled faintly, and her teeth showed up in the light of the street outside.

'I'm a bit too jumpy,' Rose said.

'I can see you are,' said Mrs Tenterden, and seemed to sense that the remark put Rose's back up, for she went on quickly: 'I didn't mean that critically, and I'd really like to help.'

77

'That's very kind of you, but I don't see how you can,' said Rose, still stiffly.

'Wives do have a little influence with husbands,' Mrs Tenterden remarked, 'and I don't think I'm any exception. Is there anything I can say to Arthur that might help? Is there any particular line of inquiry, for instance, that you would like him to follow? He told me this evening that what he really needs is a new angle, so he would be quite willing to try anything.'

Rose said more warmly: 'I'm honestly not sure. He must know about the way my father's changed, and —'

'Oh, he does.'

'Does he put it down to the strike, too?'

'Arthur is a very cautious man,' answered the detective's wife, 'and I think he regards that as a coincidence, dear. All I really want to say is that if I can help at all, I would like to.'

'You're very good, and I won't forget,' Rose said.

When she drove off she felt better, but still annoyed with herself for her early antagonism to Margaret Tenterden. She drove along the main street at about forty miles an hour, and as she left the town and switched on her headlights, put her foot down. A cyclist loomed out of the gloom, front wheel wobbling. Rose slackened speed, remembered Gordon's rebuke, and actually laughed aloud. She slowed down to thirty-five until she was out of the restricted area, then kept her speed to forty-five. It was less than five minutes' drive to the house, and she saw the lights there, as well as the lights at Soley's Farm on her left. Just beyond the turning which led to Soley's Farm and the works gates there was a sharp right turn and a steep climb, and she slowed down to take this.

As she did so, two men jumped out of the side of the road, and stood in front of the car.

Rose jammed on her brakes, her heart leaping to her throat, then thumping.

The car jolted to a standstill, the engine stalled, and she found herself breathing heavily. Then suddenly she realized that the men had scarves over their faces.

That brought vivid fear.

She stabbed at the self-starter, but the engine didn't start. The men moved towards her, one each side of the car. Two masked men, holding her up on a narrow country lane; it was

78

terrifying. She pressed the self-starter again, and prayed that it would work; the engine roared. She rammed the gear into bottom and put her foot down, but the climb was so steep that the car only crawled forward. The men disappeared from the headlamp beams, but she could see them vaguely, knew they were stretching out for the door handles. Then the door on her side was wrenched open, and a man shouted:

'Stop the engine!'

She struck out at him wildly, and thrust her foot down harder; the car jerked forward, jolting half a dozen times and throwing her backwards and forwards. The other door was wrenched open, a man clambered in beside her, stretched across her and pulled on the hand-brake.

'Get out of my car,' Rose said gaspingly. 'What do you mean by —'

The man sitting by her slid an arm round her and held her tightly, squashing one arm against his body, gripping the other so that she couldn't move. The only light came from the glow of the headlamps. She could see the men vaguely, could see the movements of the hands of the man she had struck. She was in a turmoil of fear when he raised his hand to her face. She tried to strain away, but he put his other arm at the back of her head, and held it upright; all she could do was to twist her head round from side to side, trying to free herself.

She felt something cold and sticky slap against her lips.

She heard the man say: 'You bitch,' as he let her head go. There was a sharp jolt at the back of her neck, as he struck her; it felt as if her neck was broken. She tried to open her mouth to cry out, but couldn't. She realized that the man had dabbed on adhesive plaster. She tried to bite it, but it slid off her teeth and closed on her lips and the skin about them. The man cupped his hands over her mouth with rough, painful pressure. His fingers pressed against her nostrils, so that she could hardly breathe. She fought too, her breast heaving, her whole body writhing. Then the pressure at her nostrils eased, and she heard one of the men speak.

She felt movement, and was pushed to one side. She thought that she was going to be lifted out of the MG, but instead the doors slammed and the engine started; so one of the men was at the wheel. She felt his elbow poke into her. All this time she had to fight to breathe evenly through her nostrils, a task more difficult because in the struggle she had lost so much breath. She tried to steady her thumping heart, and to understand what was happening.

The car went into reverse; so the man was taking her back from the road leading to her home. He swung round too fast; *too fast*. He jammed on the brakes and jolted her forward, but although she bumped her forehead, she was not hurt.

Her hands were free.

She knew exactly where the gear lever was, and could drive this car blindfolded; she had only to stretch out her right hand and touch the key, turn it and pull it out of the ignition, and the car would have to stop. Fear of what they planned to do with her eased away in the desperate hope of doing something to save herself. She sat a little more erect. She did not know whether the man guessed what she was going to do, but he was driving much too fast along the road to the works – past Soley's Farm and past Soley's silo.

Doris Blake had been strangled and carried up to the top of that silo and tossed down to rot.

It could happen to her!

She darted forward with her right hand, missed, and felt her fingers jab painfully against the windscreen. The driver muttered a filthy word, and brought his elbow round, jabbing her in the stomach and driving the breath out of her body. She began that awful struggle to breathe through her nostrils all over again. This time it seemed as if her lungs would burst, as if she had no chance at all; it drove away even the fear of the silo, but as she recovered, she thought of that with awful vividness. They must be near the silo, perhaps only a few hundred yards away.

She saw lights; the lights of Soley's Farm.

They dropped away behind the car. Ahead was the silo, and she pictured its round shape against the starlit sky, told herself that she could make out the height of it, then began to picture a body, *her body*, lying crumpled up on the silage.

The driver put on the brakes.

A scream rose up inside Rose, but the adhesive plaster held her lips fast, she could not make a sound.

The car was slowing down, and she thought, God, she thought, dear God don't let this happen to me, don't let it happen. Then there were other lights, bright lights straight ahead of her, and she realized that another car was coming this way, its headlights on. They dazzled her, but she could pick up the great round tower of the silo, they had been near it. The driver of the other vehicle dimmed his headlights, this driver did not dim his. The car slowed down and pulled into the side, because the road was narrow; the other 'car' was a van, she saw as it passed, but then they turned another bend, and she saw the lights of the works gate.

The car slowed down again. She sensed that it was going to turn round, and almost at once the driver swung as far to the left as he could, pulled out into the road, and reversed. He handled the car as if he was as familiar with it as she. They were headed in the other direction, back towards the silo, and the fear which had been quelled for a few minutes blazed up again.

This time, the driver did not slow down. They passed the silo. They put on speed. Rose tried to judge from the twists and turns their position on the road, but had to give it up until the engine began to roar and the car shot forward; the only part of the road straight enough for this speed was east of Corby, heading for the coast; there were about three miles of it, almost straight; she had often touched seventy along this stretch before now.

Then she was aware of light in the driving mirror, and knew that another car was coming from behind them. For a wild moment, she thought that it was a police car. It seemed to leap forward, for a second or two the cars were neck-and-neck, and she heard a man shouting. Her driver didn't call back. The other shouted again, and then swept past. She saw the tunnel of light made by its lamps, and then the bright red glow at the back of it. It swung straight in front of the MG's bonnet and stayed there, only a few yards ahead. She caught a glimpse of the radiator, but her driver said nothing, just began to put on his brakes. So did the other car driver. Both stopped, doors opened, and then footsteps sounded on the road. A man called:

'I thought I told you to make her talk.'

'You bloody fool,' said the driver of the MG, 'what good would that do? We've got to make sure she can't talk.'

'Listen! We only wanted to find out if she's discovered what —'

'That's what *you* said,' the driver interrupted. 'We can't take any chances, or she'll kill the goose that lays our golden eggs, won't she?'

81

'If you hurt her —'

'He'll be right where we want him,' the driver said confidently. 'After this he won't have a leg to stand on. What's the matter – you chicken?'

'I'm not chicken, but —' The man broke off, and then muttered: 'I suppose you're right, she'd recognize our voices, anyway.'

They were talking about *her*, as if she didn't exist, as if she couldn't hear the horror they were plotting.

12

BLOOD GROUP

ROGER WEST stretched himself as he got out of his car outside the Corby Police Station that Wednesday, five hours after he had been told that Rose Richardson was missing. The streets were almost empty, and no one took any notice of him. It was about half past three, a dead hour, and he was not sorry that there was no crowd to worry about. A uniformed policeman at the foot of the shallow flight of steps saluted, and said:

'Mr Tenterden asked you to go straight up, sir.'

'Thanks,' Roger said.

He slipped along to the cloakroom on the ground floor. He washed in cold water, combed his hair, shrugged his coat into position, and went out feeling much fresher, but still tense and on edge. He blamed himself for lost time, and felt that fierce desire to go twice as fast, because of it. He ran up the single flight of stairs to Tenterden's office, tapped, and opened the door on 'come in'. Tenterden was at his unexpectedly small, old-fashioned leather-topped desk, and Brown was at a smaller one, opposite the local man; Brown looked as if he would overlap on either side as he struggled to get up.

'Sit down,' Roger said, and shook hands briskly. 'Any news of the girl?'

'No,' said Tenterden gloomily.

'And don't ask him if he's looked in the silo,' Brown said. 'We've had twenty-seven telephone calls advising us to.'

'. . . y fools,' Tenterden muttered.

The few days had put years on him. Lines at the corners of his eyes and his lips which had not shown before now seemed deeply etched. He had a frown which pulled his lips down, and also wrinkled the skin above his nose. A lot of the stuffing seemed to have been knocked out of Arthur Tenterden.

'How about the car?' Roger asked, and sat on a corner of a typist's desk, with his back to the wall.

'Hasn't turned up,' Tenterden answered. 'But some funny things have.'

'Such as?'

'We found a lot of footprints on the road leading to Richardson's house,' said Tenterden. 'Same kind of thing as there were near the works gates, and two of the same prints. So whoever hung about the works gates the night that Jensen and Doris Blake were murdered, probably knows something about Rose Richardson.'

'Photographs of the prints?' asked Roger.

'Plenty. Took some casts, but they're overshoes.' Tenterden said.

'And we've checked the man Ragg,' Brown put in. 'We've not found any trace of overshoes or the shoes which made those prints.'

'Checked Ragg's movements last night?'

'It's being done,' Brown answered.

'Then there's another thing,' Tenterden went on. 'The last time the MG – you remember that car?'

Roger nodded.

'The last time it was seen, it was coming towards the works from Soley's Farm and the silo,' went on Tenterden. 'There was a special delivery job last night, and a young van driver named Cousins was belting along the road when the car came towards him. He says that Miss Rose had told him off for speeding yesterday morning, and the minute he realized whose car it was he slowed down. But he doesn't think she was driving. He thinks it was a man.'

'Alone?'

'He wasn't sure. The headlights had dazzled him, the chap didn't dip them.'

Roger made no comment, and Tenterden touched a notepad on his desk, and went on:

'Here's a full report, and I'm having copies made. I'm just giving you the gist of it now. Anyhow, Cousins finished his run – had to catch a train from Cranston, on the coast, to London. There's a ten-o'clock train, and he made it all right. He was allowed to park the van outside his house during the night, and reported for work as usual this morning.'

'Did he recognize the driver?'

'Couldn't even be absolutely sure it was a man, but he thought so. He says he felt sure it wasn't Miss Rose, anyhow – she would have dipped her lights.'

'Good point,' Roger said. The detail was so vital, but he

was on edge to get on more quickly, to do something himself.

'Then our chaps on the gate of the works said they saw a car coming along, thought it was coming straight up to the works, but it turned round some distance away, and followed the van. That was almost certainly the MG. But after that there isn't a trace.'

'What kind of search is being laid on?'

'I talked to Colchester, and they're doing everything they can. I've got every man on the force out searching in possible places – quarries, cliffs, one or two caves, woods, everywhere. And three parties of men from the works are out looking up in the rivers.'

'Dragging them?'

'Yes.'

Roger said: 'What about boy friends?'

'She hadn't a steady,' answered Tenterden, 'and I've questioned everyone she's danced or played tennis with lately. She's not all that man conscious, and I think her father put her off romance when he stopped the affair between her and Paul Key.'

'Checked Key?'

'He's in London.'

'Sure?'

'Well, no,' Tenterden said, and added gruffly: 'No one's reported that he's been down here, anyhow, and I'm sure that Rose Richardson's had nothing to do with him for at least a year.'

'You're probably right,' said Roger, 'but if there was more in it than Richardson thought, they might have been meeting on the quiet. Browny, you ring the Yard and check whether Paul Key's at his home.'

Brown lifted a receiver.

'Has Sir Lancelot Key been down?' asked Roger.

'He came down for the weekend, stayed here yesterday, and went back this morning,' answered Tenterden.

'Looks like a painting out of Van Dyck, goatee beard and all,' volunteered Brown, and then said into the telephone: 'Get me the Yard will you? – Chief Inspector Cope.' He replaced his receiver.

'I don't know about Van Dyck,' said Tenterden, 'but most

85

people get a bit of a shock when they see Sir Lancelot. He's more like a popular idea of a painter than a printer.'

Roger said: 'And he's back in London.'

'Yes.'

'How about the blood on those spools?' asked Roger, and then the telephone bell rang. Brown was passing on to Cope the instructions which Roger had given him, while Tenterden was saying quietly:

'It's almost certainly Jensen's, Handsome. Group C, like Jensen's, and as far as we can get from Arnold, several days old. But there's something even more definite.' He stretched out for a cardboard box, took the lid off, and with great care shook out a damaged spool, smeared with brown. As Roger took this gingerly, he saw what the Corby man meant; there were at least four hairs stuck on here. He touched a hair with his forefinger; it was almost jet black, and had a tendency to curl.

'Jensen's?'

'Yes, for certain.'

'So the weapon used to kill Jensen was used to smash the spools.'

'Yes.'

'It still doesn't let Blake out,' Roger argued, almost stubbornly. 'He might have a good hate against the firm. There's been this bother between him and Richardson.' When Tenterden didn't answer, Roger grinned, and went on: 'I know, he would have had to have a brainstorm. How is Blake?'

'Haven't seen him since he was taken up to Colchester,' said Tenterden. 'I'm told he won't eat, just sits and mopes in his cell. I don't have to point out that Blake couldn't have spirited Rose Richardson away, do I?' asked Tenterden. 'And I don't —'

A telephone bell rang and Tenterden broke off at the same moment as Brown finished with the Yard. He lifted his receiver, frowned, said: 'Yes, all right,' and put the receiver down. He frowned as he reported: 'It's Richardson. He's on his way up. I warn you, he's almost violent. Try not to —'

There was a clatter of footsteps on the stairs, then the door was thrust open and banged against the wall. Sydney Richardson strode in, and Roger was appalled at his appearance. Now his eyes glittered wildly, and he had no colour at all. Roger was reminded vividly of Charlie Blake; here was a man who

86

hadn't slept for a long time. Richardson strode into the room, stared at Tenterden, began to speak, and then spun round on Roger.

'*Have you found my daughter?*'

'Mr Richardson —' Tenterden began.

'You keep quiet. I'm talking to West. *Have you found my daughter?*'

'No, Mr Richardson, but —'

'When are you going to find her? Why are you sitting on your backsides instead of being out looking for her? *Answer me that!*' he screeched. 'Why are you sitting on your backsides —'

Roger was standing between Tenterden and Brown, and Richardson thrust himself forward, hands stretched out as if he would strike him. Tenterden muttered something in the back of his throat. A woman whom Roger had not seen before appeared in the doorway; all he knew was that on sight he felt sorry for her.

'Mr Richardson —' Brown was stung to say, 'we've got the police forces of two counties, private search parties and —'

'Words, words, words!' Now the man was standing just in front of Roger; if he moved farther forward they were bound to collide. 'I insist on knowing why you're squatting here in this room instead of being out looking for my daughter. *Are you going to tell me or aren't you?*'

He flung his hands out, and touched Roger on the chest.

The woman in the doorway said in a whispering voice: 'Sydney, don't.'

Roger dropped his right hand to Richardson's left, gripped his wrist, twisted, and sent him staggering back. He struck a chair with the back of his legs, and would have fallen but for the wall. He looked dazed, and the wildness eased a little out of his eyes.

The woman said: 'Arthur, he's not himself, you know that.'

'We know, Mrs Richardson,' Tenterden said.

Richardson whispered. 'We've got to find Rose. We've got to find Rose.'

'I'm sure the police are doing all they can,' his wife said unhappily. 'If there's any news, they'll tell us. I'm sure they will.'

'Of course, Mrs Richardson,' Tenterden said.

'We might stand a better chance of finding Miss Richardson

and of saving her life if Mr Richardson would tell us everything he knows,' said Roger coldly. 'If we find her body, explanations would be too late.'

He stopped abruptly. No one else spoke. Even Tenterden and Brown stared at him uncomprehendingly, and from the doorway Richardson's wife stood open-mouthed, her hands raised to her breast, as if in shock. Richardson straightened up from the wall, moistened his lips, and said to Roger:

'I've nothing to blame myself for. *You're* to blame. You knew there was danger, and you let this happen to her.'

'We didn't know there was any danger to your daughter,' said Roger. 'Did you?' When Richardson didn't answer, he went a step forward and demanded roughly: 'Come on, let's have the truth. Did you know? What's eating you? What's on your mind?'

'He didn't know —' Mrs Richardson began.

Roger rasped: 'Quiet, please!'

Richardson was sweating now, and his eyes closed.

'I don't know what —' he began, stopped, opened his eyes and stared at Roger, and muttered: 'I don't know what you're talking about.'

'You know,' Roger said, still roughly. 'What's on your mind, Richardson? Two people have been murdered, your own daughter might be dead at this moment, attempts have been made to sabotage the works, and you know what it's all about. As soon as you tell us we'll have a chance of finding out who's behind it, and why it's happening.'

There was a short, tense silence, and in it Richardson moved slowly back to the wall, as if in need of support. Everyone was staring at him, no one could doubt that in his desperation he would talk.

Then a telephone bell blared out, breaking the tension. Tenterden glanced at it, but didn't move towards it. The bell rang again, harshly. Richardson covered his face with his hands, and his wife went towards him. The bell rang for a third time. Tenterden said: 'Damn the thing,' and picked up the receiver. 'Tenterden,' he announced.

Then, he gasped: *'Where is it?'* and on that instant everyone in the office swivelled round towards him.

13

CLIFF FALL

THE GLITTER was back in Richardson's eyes, and he had a pin point of scarlet on each cheek. His wife was clutching his arm now, but looking at Tenterden, whose eyes were glistening, whose knuckles were gleaming white where he gripped the telephone.

'Right,' he said, and put the receiver down with a bang. He drew a deep breath. 'The car's been seen at Bracken Head,' he went on, with slow vehemence. 'Men are being lowered to it now.' After a pause he explained to Roger and Brown: 'It's a cliff headland about thirty miles from here.'

'Rose —' began Mrs Richardson.

'By the time we get there we shall know whether your daughter's in the car,' said Tenterden. 'I think you and Mr Richardson had better come in a police car, Mrs Richardson – unless you would rather wait until there's definite news.'

'I'd – I'd like to come,' Mrs Richardson muttered. She looked almost as broken as her husband, timid, frightened, despairing.

'Oh, God,' Richardson gasped, and the words sounded more like prayer than blasphemy. 'Let her be safe. Let her be safe.' He swung towards the door, the moment of breakdown and perhaps confession gone, hope pouring into him and giving him strength. He did not wait for his wife, and she almost ran after him.

'Let him drive himself,' Roger said. 'I'll come in your car, Arthur. I've done enough driving for today.'

'Suits me,' said Tenterden. 'I'll lay on a few odds and ends.' He talked into the telephone for less than thirty seconds, brisk and efficient where action and routine were required, then moved with the others towards the door. A telephone rang on Brown's desk, and he went back to answer it. Roger went with Tenterden, whose big car was in the yard by the side of the police station. By the time he had the engine started, Brown was alongside him, puffing.

'That was Cope,' he reported. 'Paul Key's been in London this week, and he and his brother and father are on the way down here. Because of their cousin's disappearance, Cope understands.'

'Thanks,' said Roger. None of the report had any immediate significance, and he noted it automatically.

As they started out from Corby, Tenterden said: 'Bracken Head's a notorious suicide spot, and there have been three cases of cars going over it in the last few years. Tricky place, as you'll see when we get there. Several gorges in the cliffs, and the bottom of them is under water up to about twenty feet at high tide.' He swung past a Richardson and Key delivery van at the approach to the station, and said: 'There's young Cousins, who saw the car last night.'

Roger had caught a glimpse of a big-eyed, fair-haired youth.

'So if the car went over the edge last night, it's been under twenty feet of water at least once,' he said.

'Probably,' answered Tenterden.

Brown hammered the obvious home hard.

'So if she was in it, she's had it,' he said. 'What do you think her father will do then, Handsome?'

'I think he could explain what's driving him off his head,' Roger said.

A dozen cars were drawn up close to the edge of the cliffs at Bracken Head, and a fire engine, backed on to the edge, showed up vivid scarlet in the afternoon sun. At least thirty people stood about, many of them policemen, a few of them people whom Roger had recognized at the works. Farmer Sam Soley was there in a big old Austin. Richardson was standing so close to the edge that it looked as if his wife and another man, a small man whom Roger did not recognize from a distance, were trying to hold him back. Roger got out of the car as Tenterden pulled up, Brown squeezed himself out on the other side, and all three walked briskly towards the fire escape. As they drew nearer they could see stakes driven into the ground with ropes drawn taut from them to the cliff edge.

Richardson was saying: 'I've got to go down, I tell you.'

The little man was Dr Arnold.

'I wish you'd have more sense,' the doctor said testily, and startled Roger; few people in Corby were likely to talk to Richardson like that. 'You're harassing everyone and making their job more difficult.'

Richardson seemed to sag.

A tall, lean man, Salmon, Tenterden's chief *aide* and a competent detective, came from the edge of the cliff where he had been looking over. He had corn-coloured hair and very thin features, and his nose was pushed a little to one side.

'Any report yet?' asked Tenterden.

'No,' Salmon answered. 'Afternoon, Mr West. The car's in a damned awkward position, more by luck than judgement that anyone saw it. This is the best spot for getting down, but the best viewpoint is over there.' He led the way towards the fringe of the crowd, to a spot where three men were standing, each with a camera. It hadn't taken long for the news to spread, Roger reflected grimly, and he glanced round at Richardson, who seemed to have collapsed.

In this crisis, his wife appeared to find more strength, as if she were bracing herself for both their sakes.

'There it is,' Salmon announced.

Roger stared down the side of the rugged cliff. He was acutely conscious of the fact that all three cameras were training on him as he saw the small red car. It was at least three hundred feet below him, and had fallen into a kind of ravine and become jammed between big mounds on either side. Below it the sea, whipped by a brisk east wind, was seething about the cliff base and racing into a small, sandy cove. In places, the headland was sheer, and it jutted right out into the North Sea, so that it was impossible to see the rest of the coast when one stood on that tip.

The sun glistened on the blue water, the white froth of the waves, the scarlet of the pathetic-looking little car – and on three men, each climbing over the broken foot of the cliffs. Seaweed was making the clay and sand slippery, and each of the men wore rubber boots, which did not help foothold. They were some fifty yards from the car, as far as Roger could judge, but before they could reach it they had to climb a dozen steep ridges, each twenty or thirty feet high, and it would probably be ten or fifteen minutes before they looked into the car. Undoubtedly the firemen had selected the best place to lower them, however; the cliff over which the MG had fallen was overhanging and dangerous, and Roger saw that there were big cracks in it; the weight of a man could cause an avalanche, and even now there was some danger of falling clay and sandstone.

The three men looked like midgets.

A car came crawling towards Roger and the others, and a Corby policeman said:

'They've got radio down there, sir, they'll report as soon as they've looked inside the car.'

'How long have we got before the tide comes in?' asked Roger.

'Couple of hours yet,' said Tenterden, 'but as far as I can see from here, the car didn't get down to the high-water mark. What do you think, Salmon?'

'Shouldn't think it did,' answered the other man. 'About ten feet above it, I'd say. Not that it makes much difference if Rose Richardson's in there. The crash would kill her.'

For ten interminable minutes the crowd stood watching, the three firemen crept and crawled over the ridges, and yet seemed to get no nearer. But they were nearer. Roger saw the walkie-talkie radio unit strapped to one man's back – the man nearest the car. He watched everyone near him, and sensed the acuteness of their anxiety. Everyone who knew Rose Richardson had liked her, had been fond of her; and there was not a man here who did not think that she was dead. Her father and mother were now standing between the fire engine and Roger, Richardson staring down, the woman's face set and bleak, Arnold between them.

A car engine sounded high and fast, and an Allard swung off the road and on to the headland. It stopped near the Richardson's, and three men got out. The first was dapper and bearded, and Roger placed him at once as Sir Lancelot Key. The other two men were younger, one short, stocky, and fair, the other tall, good-looking, and very dark.

'Strewth, there's Paul Key!' Salmon exclaimed. 'Haven't seen him for years!'

'The dark one?' Roger asked.

'Yes.'

'The black sheep of the Key family,' Brown said, and then demanded edgily: 'Why the hell don't they get a move on down there?'

'Sharp as a razor, those rocks,' explained Tenterden. 'Used

to climb them when I was a boy. What was the record time to get across, Salmon?'

'Forty-nine minutes in my time, sir.'

'They've been about half an hour,' said Tenterden. 'I – hallo, he's over.' They saw the man with the walkie-talkie move much more quickly, as if he were no longer handicapped by the slippery ridges. The other two were some distance behind him, but this man went quite quickly, holding on wherever he could for support, but without seeming to be in any danger of falling.

He touched the car and looked in.

Tenterden drew in a hissing breath.

The man who had driven up behind them clicked on the radio, and little sounds came through, as of the man touching the door of the car, opening it, slipping on the ridges. Then a voice came clearly:

'Fireman Cartwright speaking, sir. Can you hear me?'

Another man said: 'Yes, Cartwright, we can hear you.'

'I'm leaning inside the car,' Cartwright said. The tension even among those near Roger seemed to reach screaming point. Richardson was standing absolutely erect, with his hands clenched, Sir Lancelot Key was by his side, and Key's two sons were on either side of Mrs Richardson. Then the fireman said in a matter-of-fact voice: 'It's Miss Richardson all right, sir.'

Someone gasped.

Cartwright went on in that unbelievably casual voice:

'She has adhesive plaster over her mouth, as if to prevent her from crying out, the cold-blooded devil.' Cartwright disappeared inside the car, but his voice came back just as clearly. 'I am sitting by the side of Miss Richardson, sir, and I have reason to believe—'

He broke off.

What the hell had he reason to believe?

'—that life is not extinct,' Cartwright announced calmly. 'I detect slight movement at the chest. I am about to check the pulse.' There was an agony of silence, while men stared at each other unbelievingly; and Roger saw Dr Arnold leave Richardson and his party, and go towards the fire engine.

Cartwright said: 'The pulse is faint but regular, sir. I think we ought to have a doctor down here at once.'

Another voice came, brisk and efficient, and quite as matter-of-fact as Cartwright's.

'Cartwright, this is Dr Arnold. Can you hear me?'

'Yes, sir.'

'Have you surgical spirit in your first-aid kit?'

'Yes, sir.'

'Use this to dab over the adhesive plaster, allow it to soak in, and then pull the plaster away gently.'

'I know how to do it, sir.'

'Right. Get that done first, in order to improve the facilities for breathing. Report when the plaster's off.'

'Very good, sir.'

'My God,' Salmon said tensely. 'She's alive.'

'Wonder what Richardson —' Tenterden began, and then he broke off. Roger glanced swiftly towards the spot where the Richardsons and the Keys were standing, and saw Mrs Richardson go forward, hands outstretched. He heard her cry: *'Syd!'* Sir Lancelot Key grabbed her arm. Richardson reached the edge of the cliff, turned his back on the sea, and started to climb down. One moment his tall, angular figure was stark against the sky, the next only his head and shoulders appeared; and then they vanished. The Key brothers went running towards the edge, and Tenterden said:

'He'll kill himself.'

'Could be,' said Roger. 'But we want to get down there, too. We want that car checked for prints and anything else we might find, and we've only got two hours of daylight. I'm going.' It was a relief to say that, a relief to get some physical action; it was almost as if he wanted to flagellate himself. 'You and Brown aren't built for it, Arthur. How about you, Salmon?'

'I'm game, sir.'

'Good. My case is in the boot of your car, Arthur. I'd better have it strapped on my back.' They were moving towards Tenterden's car, and Roger went on: 'Salmon, nip ahead and tell the Chief Fire Officer that we're going down on those ropes.'

'Right away,' Salmon said.

'Handsome, are you sure you ought —?' began Brown.

'Yes,' said Roger curtly.

'That's the trouble with you, never happy unless you're risking your neck,' Brown muttered. 'I don't mind admitting I wouldn't go down there for a fortune.'

'You can come and pick up my pieces,' Roger said, but

broke off when Cartwright's voice was broadcast again. The tension which everyone felt was in the very air, like something which could be cut.

'The plaster is off, sir, and very little skin damage has been caused.'

'Good,' said Arnold. 'Now you can check if it is safe to move the patient. Look for any signs of broken bones, any sign of internal injury, any —'

'I know the drill, sir.'

'Damned good man, that Cartwright,' Salmon said.

'Very well.' Arnold spoke as officially as if he were in the morgue. 'Once you are satisfied that no harm will come to the patient if you move her before I arrive, get her out of the vehicle, and lay her on a piece of flat rock,' he said. 'In your considered opinion, will it be better to bring her back up the cliff, or by boat?'

'By boat, sir. We can get her down easy enough, but I wouldn't like to chance bringing her up.'

'Very good,' said Arnold, and then turned to the Chief Fire Officer and said in a voice which only just sounded over the loudspeaker, 'I shall go down at once. You will arrange for a launch immediately, won't you?'

'Two are on the way,' said the Chief Fire Officer. 'I fixed that with the police.'

'Good,' said Arnold, and he slipped a harness over his shoulders and clipped the harness on to the rope, showing that he had been studying the way to get down the cliff-side, and that he was not going to waste a moment. He was beginning to climb over, facing the face of the cliff, when Roger saw a little cloud of dust rise up, and then heard a sharp crack of sound.

Arnold stopped.

Someone shouted: 'The cliff's falling!'

Then Roger saw that Richardson, only a few yards down the cliff edge, was clinging to an overhanging piece of rock, and that part of this had fallen and was bouncing down the cliff side. If it struck a sandy patch it might start an avalanche; it could even bury the men down there, the unconscious girl, and even the car.

'We'd better get Richardson back first,' he said, and swung round towards the spot where the man had climbed over.

'He's not worth breaking your neck for!' Brown protested. 'If he falls serve him bloody well right.'

'He could do a lot of damage,' Roger pointed out, 'and he might be an invaluable witness. I —'

He heard a scream; and he saw Richardson fall.

14

DUMB WITNESSES

ROGER WATCHED the man as he fell, saw him strike an overhanging piece of hard clay, which checked his fall and flung him sideways. Richardson was only about thirty yards away, and Roger could see the man's expression, knew that he was in terror, but knew also that he hadn't lost his head. He snatched at a small bush growing out of the face of the cliff, and clutched it. He stopped falling. The small stones and rubble which tumbled downwards were making a lot of noise, but did not seem to dislodge any other stones.

Young Peter Key was on his stomach leaning over the edge, obviously trying to reach Richardson, who was still yards away. The taller, black-haired Paul Key kept well away from the cliff, while bearded Sir Lancelot kept an arm round Richardson's wife, to hold her back.

The two firemen below were staring upwards, as if afraid of what might follow. Cartwright was already out of the car, but what he said over the walkie-talkie was distorted, partly by the new rumbling.

Arnold was now lowering himself hand over fist, as if determined not to allow the disturbance to worry him.

'If we can get a rope round Richardson he'll be all right,' said Tenterden. 'The roots look safe enough.' He stared at the way the roots were being strained from the cliff, but they showed no sign of giving way.

Two firemen came up, carrying a coil of rope, and Peter Key moved away and dusted himself down.

'With a bit of luck, we'll soon have him up,' one of the firemen said, and looked as if he wanted to add what he thought of Sydney Richardson. Richardson had hitched himself to one side so that he couldn't fall so easily, and there was less strain on the bush. It seemed obvious that he had at last realized that he could not hope to climb down; there was nothing like the shadow of death to put sense into a man. 'Only danger is loose earth,' the little fireman added. 'If any more falls, it'll go straight down on top of that car.'

As he spoke, the Chief Fire Officer came up, and said to Tenterden:

'We ought to move all these cars back at least twenty yards. If the soil's been loosened there could be a nasty fall.'

'I'll lay it on,' Tenterden promised, and sent a man for the drivers of the cars which were too close to the edge.

The little fireman and his companion climbed over cautiously, and Roger watched as they put a rope round Richardson. With one man on either side of him, they began to help him up, while Salmon, Brown, Peter Key, and two Corby policemen took the strain on the ropes. So much was happening at once that it would be easy to miss the most important, and Roger, inwardly fuming because he had been delayed, watched the fireman down by the car, and Arnold being lowered.

The girl had been lifted out by the men.

She had been put on to a stretcher, and even from here it was easy to see how cautiously the men were handling her. It would be some time before they managed to get her over the ridges to the shore, but she would soon be out of sight from the cliff. The stuttering noise of a motor launch became audible, and two launches appeared round the headland, moving very fast; there were three men in each.

Up here there was a noise of engines as several cars were started at once, their owners moving them out of the danger zone. Soley, Paul Key, and two newspapermen were the only ones whom Roger noticed. Engines snarled as the cars were reversed up the sloping land.

One of the newspapermen with a camera came up, and asked:

'Wouldn't care to estimate the cost of an operation like this, Mr West, would you?'

Roger forced a smile. 'I'd rather leave the guessing to you.'

'Any idea what happened to Miss Richardson yet?'

'No.'

'Must be attempted murder, in view of that adhesive plaster.' The newspaperman was young, curly haired, and probably only pretending to be naïve.

'Could be,' agreed Roger mildly, and then Richardson was lifted over the top. His coat was badly torn, one of his shoes had a gash in it, and dust and dirt smothered his hair and made him look almost like a black man. Two nasty scratches over his eyes were bleeding, and there was a little scratch on his chin. He kept spitting out dirt.

'Rope's free now,' Salmon said suddenly.

He could talk to Richardson at once, Roger knew, but probably it would do little good. It would be impossible to question the man privately, and it wouldn't be reasonable to take him away from here until they had a fuller report on his daughter's condition. Richardson would probably never be in a more vulnerable position for questioning, even if he did know anything of importance, but the time simply wasn't right. Roger satisfied himself with saying:

'We'll want to talk to Mr Richardson again before he goes back home, Superintendent.'

'I'll arrange it,' Tenterden promised, and then Brown, who looked very cold on the windswept headland, and miserable with it, came over and joined Roger. He kept his voice low as he said:

'I don't think you ought to go down there.'

'Forget it, Browny.'

'I still don't think you ought to go,' said Brown doggedly. 'I've been having a good look at this cliff, and there are a dozen places where it might collapse. Been too many people up here today, and too much moving about. Won't need much to start a nasty fall, and if that happened you could have had it.'

Roger said: 'Someone's got to go down.'

'Well, maybe, but —'

'Forget it,' Roger said again.

But as he fastened on the shoulder harness by the fire engine, and watched Salmon doing the same, he felt a twinge of disquiet. There were cracks — not in the top of the cliff, but in the cliff face itself. There were evidences of heavy falls in different spots, too, and for the first time he noticed a sign which read: *Danger – Keep Back*. The sun was unexpectedly warm on the back of his head. When he started down, he saw the sea breaking more roughly on the foot of the cliffs, and the wind seemed gustier here than it had on the top. He felt surprisingly lonely, too. He could not be more than thirty or forty feet way from the cliff-top, but could see no one up there, and only Salmon was with him. Then Salmon's harness got stuck on the rope.

'You carry on, sir,' he said. 'I'll get free in a minute.'

'Right,' said Roger.

If he slipped, his harness would hold him, he told himself. But ropes could break. The case, his murder bag, was heavy on his back, and the harness was chafing him under his right arm. When he looked down again he was half-way between the top of the cliff and the nearest of the rocks where he would free himself from the harness, and start climbing.

He could not see the car from here, or the boat party, but could see Arnold, climbing over ridges which had given Cartwright so much trouble. Now and again, his own rope seemed to go slack, and once it was jerked sharply, and flung him against the side of the cliff painfully. He dangled for a few seconds, then started to go down again, feet planted against the surface of the cliff. Small showers of stones and dirt fell ahead of him. A heavier shower came from above, and he closed his eyes and turned his head away sharply, but could not stop some of the dust getting into his eyes. His eyes watered freely, but he kept going down, and then kicked against a ridge of earth immediately beneath him. He dabbed his eyes with his handkerchief; they were painful, but he could see, and the surrounding danger gave a strange quiet to his mind.

Salmon, who had caused the fall of dust, was still half-way up to the top. He himself was isolated except for the two launches bobbing up and down on the sea; they were waiting for the girl. He caught sight of a litttle dinghy, and that told him that the sea was too rough for the launches to come right in. It would be difficult to get a stretcher on to that dinghy.

He stood upright, freed himself from the harness, and then clambered over the ridges. The clay was slippery with seaweed, and had been worn smooth by countless tides. The worst part came when he had nothing to hold on to, but soon he was able to steady himself. From here, he could see the car more clearly – and he saw two men going very slowly down towards the little sandy inlet where the dinghy was drawn up. Dr Arnold was walking just behind the stretcher.

Roger called: 'Dr Arnold!'

The little man looked round.

'How is she?' Roger called.

'I have every reason to hope that she will survive,' Arnold said. 'I will discuss it with you later.' He nodded brusquely, and turned and followed the stretcher, and for the first time since he had started to climb down, Roger grinned; he would for ever have a soft spot for the pompous little police surgeon. Arnold wouldn't talk loosely, either; there must be a real chance that the girl would recover, and therefore that she would be able to give them some information; she might even have recognized her attackers.

But she might not come round for some time.

Roger reached the car. One fireman was left on duty there, the smallest of them all. Roger offered him a cigarette, and they lit up, while Roger opened his case, took out his magnifying glass, and made a quick examination of the inside of the car. A glass didn't help to perform miracles but often came in handy. He saw pieces of grit, paper, a cigarette end, some shreds of tobacco, a broken point of a pencil, some threads of linen. There were some scratches on the old black leather upholstery, and these seemed new. One of the remarkable things was the fact that the car had been comparatively little damaged, and the girl was doubtless alive because of that. He looked upwards, studying the trajectory of the fall. He could just make out the broken cliff where the car had plunged over, and it so happened that the face of the cliff had sloped very gradually from the spot where the wheels had struck it; another car would probably have landed on its back, and if that had happened, the girl would almost certainly have been killed. As it was, by a freak of balance the MG had fallen on its wheels again, and then actually run about fifty or sixty yards until it had struck some heavy sandstone ridges. It had been stuck between one tall ridge and a small one, and jammed tightly; but for that it would have gone well below sea-level.

Rose Richardson would never have more luck than she had had this time.

Salmon came up.

'Having any luck?' he asked.

'Don't know,' said Roger, 'but I think we ought to use a powder and see if we can get any more prints from the wheel. Then we can check the floor for bits and pieces. I'll do the wheel and the gear lever, you start on the floor, will you?'

'Right,' said Salmon. 'Mind if I borrow your tweezers and some envelopes?'

'Help yourself,' Roger said. He leaned through the driving door and breathed on the black ebonite wheel, so that any finger-prints on it would show up. Several did, but most of them were smeared, and he felt pretty certain that whoever had handled the car had worn gloves. He checked the handle of the gear lever, and there was hardly a print on it. He grunted but said nothing about his disappointment as he tried the dashboard.

'Anything doing?' asked Salmon.

'Not much,' Roger said. 'I think we ought to take this steering-wheel off and take it up, though, we might —'

He broke off.

He heard a rushing sound, and distant shouting. He glanced up in alarm, and saw the front wheels and the nose of a car leap on to the edge of the cliff, just about the spot where the MG had fallen over.

He heard Salmon cry: *'My God!'*

'Scramble!' Roger gasped, and flung himself away from the side of the car. The rushing noise stopped suddenly, but there were different sounds, of rending, crashing noises. The car had come right over the edge. It looked like an enormous caterpillar when he saw the undercarriage, but suddenly and with bewildering precision it began to turn over. It struck the cliff face again. A big rock was dislodged and came crashing down. Roger reached a smooth spot, the patch the ambulance men had used, and went into a skid. He waved his arms wildly, held his balance, and then leapt downwards towards the sand. The dinghy was already being towed along behind one of the launches, the first launch was out of sight.

The car crashed into the MG. A great fall of dirt and stones was smothering it and the small car – burying them, burying his case of instruments and all the hope there was of finding clues here.

Then Roger realized that Salmon was almost buried, too.

15

BURIAL

ROGER SAW the whole scene with frightening clarity.

He had been on the left of the MG and nearer this sand and escape. The avalanche caused by the other car had fallen mostly on the far side, and Salmon had been trapped before he could get far enough away. Now, his head and one arm showed, obviously he was trying desperately to keep more stones from falling on to his head, but he had no chance at all, for there was a steady fall in a kind of cascade; every second buried him more deeply. The two cars were half buried, too, and obviously there was a danger that the big one on top of the MG might topple over. If it did, there would be no chance for Salmon.

Only his hand showed, and there was no sign at all of the little fireman.

Roger glanced round at the sea. The dinghy had turned the headland, and was out of sight; it had probably been out of earshot, too. He was utterly alone, with the whippy wind and the writhing sea swarming up so that he was ankle deep in water.

He started back for the half-buried cars and the mound of soil and clay. Salmon's hand was motionless. Roger looked round desperately for something to dig with, but there was nothing. He clambered up the rock towards Salmon, and reached a spot just in front of the hand. He knelt down in the loose soil and rock and began to dig with his hands, forcing himself to make each movement deliberate. Stones were sharp against the tips of his fingers and his nails, but that did not worry him. Ominous creaking noises did. The big car, now on its side, was an old Austin, and it was perched precariously above the MG. If it toppled forward it would fall on him and on Salmon, whose hand had stopped moving. Roger kept looking round, but there was still no sign of the little fireman.

He kept digging; and the groaning, creaking noise was repeated time and time again. Whenever he glanced up, the undercarriage of the car seemed to be nearer, as if everything was slipping. The awful thing was the depth to which Salmon was buried, and the difficulty of moving the earth which kept running back into the hole made by his hands. Roger pressed against the sides, to try to stop it. Soon he had about eighteen inches clear, and he felt something hard and yet different from the stones. A moment later he saw Salmon's brown hair and the top of his forehead. He scooped the earth away with great care, first clearing the man's eyes, then his nostrils. Salmon's eyes were tightly closed, and rimmed with dirt. His nostrils were blocked, and there was a lot of black earth in his mouth. Roger dug, still carefully, until the whole of the head was clear – and as he did so, he saw that there was a slight convulsive kind of movement at the man's throat.

Salmon had a chance, provided he could be freed and given artificial respiration, but the chances of getting him out of here were almost negligible; it would take hours to pull him free, and if he were cleared the car would almost certainly crash on top of them.

Roger stood up, and eased his aching back, but there was no time to rest. The gaping underbelly of the big old car was very close to his head, and the only chance of preventing it from falling was to support it with clayey soil, and it would take him a long time to do that. It might be possible to push it farther on top of the MG, but there was always the danger that if he did that it would dislodge the smaller car – and bury him and Salmon completely.

What the hell should he do?

He seemed absolutely remote from the world. He could not see the top of the cliff because of the overhanging car, and behind him the sea was splashing much higher than it had been even half an hour before. There was a howl of wind, too, lashing at the water, lashing at Roger; it was bitterly cold.

He seemed to stand still for an age, but it was only a few agonizing seconds, while he decided what he ought to do.

The obvious thing, the only safe thing for himself, was to get away from here and climb ten or twenty yards up the cliff. If he did that, he would be quite safe from falling soil and sand, from the cars, from all of the obvious dangers; and sooner or later someone would come down for him. Someone was probably on the way now, but it would take a long time, and there had undoubtedly been a big cliff fall in the wake of that car.

Who had allowed it to roll forward?

The question came in and out of his mind as he knelt down again, glancing up at the sanctuary of the cliff ridges not far to his left, and ten yards above him. Of course, he couldn't leave Salmon. But as he began to dig again, and heard the creaking and the groaning of the earth under the weight of the cars, he found himself clenching his teeth. Mind pictures of Janet and the boys became vivid and compelling. Janet seemed to be saying: *'You can't help them, come away while you can.'* And wasn't that true? Was there any way in which he could help Salmon and the fireman? Wasn't he simply throwing away his own life in a forlorn attempt at saving these men? It was one thing to be a hero, but to throw one's life away was madness. He owed Janet and the boys more than that. *He owed Janet and the boys more than that!* The wind was like ice on his back, and yet sweat was dripping off his forehead.

He heard a crunch of sound.

He darted back, stubbed his toes into the earth, and could not go any farther. Staring upwards, he saw the gaping chassis dropping towards him, slowly, menacingly, and there was absolutely nothing he could do.

It stopped.

He wiped the sweat off his forehead, and paused in his digging, looking at Salmon's pale, dirty streaked face. The man was dead. He, Roger, was simply making a fool of himself. What was the use of trying to save a dead man? Once he attempted to pull Salmon up it would loosen so much more of the fallen dirt and rock, that the car would come right down on him. It was already almost touching him when he stood up.

He went on digging.

Then, from behind him, he heard a shout. He did not turn round swiftly, for he was afraid of making any sudden movement, but his heart began to pound. The man shouted again. He did not know who it was, but assumed that it was one of the firemen; several of them might be hurrying down the ropes he and Salmon had used; they wouldn't have any harness, but it was comparatively easy to climb down.

'Can you hear me?' the man called.

'I can hear you,' Roger called back.

'Can you get free?'

'There's a man buried alive,' Roger said quietly.

'What's needed to get him out?' The stranger's voice was

calm and detached, reminding him of Dr Arnold, but this wasn't Arnold, it was a younger man.

Roger called: 'Why don't you come and see?'

'There are two of us here. Tell us what you want, and one of us will go back for it.'

Thank God for a man of intelligence.

'All right,' called Roger. 'The car which fell over the cliff is balanced just above Miss Richardson's MG, and only some loose earth is stopping it from falling. If it falls, it will bury me as well as the other man – Salmon.'

'Who?'

'Never mind. We need spades, shovels, and something to shore up the earth and stop the car from falling. I don't think there's much time.'

'I follow,' the man said. 'We'll fix it. Are you all right for a while?'

'Yes.'

There was a murmur of voices, then sounds of footsteps as someone scrambled up the cliff-side beyond the ridges which separated them from Roger. Roger began to dig again, putting all the loose earth behind Salmon's head, building up a little more resistance to the slow, remorseless droop of the car.

Then he heard the scrambling footsteps close by, and the man who had called out spoke from just behind him.

'Won't be half a jiff.' He was still reassuringly calm. 'I can size the situation up better from here.' There was a long pause. 'With a bit of luck, if we could lift some clay soil between us, we could tilt that Old Reliable the other way, and get us out of a lot of trouble. Are the chap's nose and mouth clear?'

'Clear as I can get them.'

'If you back about four paces, and then move over to the left, you'll see what I mean,' the stranger said.

Roger backed cautiously, a long step at a time. With each, his foot went ankle deep in earth, but he could free his foot without difficulty. Then he stepped on to firmer ground, and turned round to see who was here.

This was young Peter Key, whom he had seen on the headland with his father and brother only half an hour ago. This was the quiet and the so-called unimaginative son. His fair hair was unruffled, his fresh complexion was clear and healthy, and he had very clear grey eyes. He was not really good looking, but there was something wholesome about him, and

106

oddly, something a little dull, that showed in the set of his rather large chin, and in the expression in his eyes. He was in complete command of himself and the situation, and nothing was likely to put him off his stroke. He couldn't be more than twenty-six or seven, Roger judged.

He soon saw what young Key meant.

Seen from here, the big old Austin showed up in different perspective. It had now reached a corner of the roof of the MG and, at the moment, was almost balancing on that corner and tipping down towards Roger, Key, and Salmon. If sufficiently heavy soil could be pushed into the right position any danger of it falling farther towards them would be gone; then they could safely put their weight against it at one corner and push it backwards. There was a risk that it would dislodge the MG, but from what he recalled of the original position of the smaller car, it would take a lot of dislodging.

'See what I mean?' said Peter Key.

'Yes,' said Roger. 'Let's get on with it.'

'Right, Superintendent,' Key said, much as he might have said, 'Yes, sir,' in his days of military service.

It took them ten minutes of heaving and straining to get the rocks into position, another five to push the big car back so that there was no danger from it. Then, together, they began to dig Salmon out. He was free to the waist when two more firemen, two policemen carrying spades, wooden stakes, ropes, and a pulley arrived, and soon Salmon was stretched out on a flat ledge, being given artificial respiration. The hopeless digging began for the little fireman. More men arrived, and then a launch carrying half a dozen men and more equipment came close inshore, and the men waded to the ridges, which were now half submerged.

By then, daylight was fading.

'Don't know whether we'll save Salmon, but if we don't you won't be able to blame yourself,' said Peter Key. 'Bloody awful business. I've known Salmon since I was knee high. Used to help me across the road when I was let out on my own to buy ice-cream.' His clear eyes were hard and frosty. 'And the fireman's an old Corby chap, too. Superintendent, I know you're all in, and this is hardly the time to harass you, but we want the swine who did this. I want a hand in catching him, too – especially for what he did to Rose.' He seemed suddenly to be talking to himself as he spoke of Richardson's daughter, and there was a different expression in his eyes; a softening.

Roger said: 'What's the latest news of her?'

'I don't know any more than you do. She'll be in Kemble Hospital by now, I hope. If they killed her —' He broke off.

Roger said: 'Do you know of anyone with a motive for killing her?'

'I do not. Nor does anyone in Corby. There isn't a woman more liked —' Peter Key broke off, having declared his feelings so clearly, and when he went on it was in a harsher voice: 'The man must be mad.'

'It could be,' said Roger. His head was aching badly, his back seemed ready to break, and his legs wanted to double up beneath him. The thought of hoisting himself up on that rope was repugnant, but it had to be faced. Then he asked the question which had been nagging at the back of his mind since the big old car had first come crashing down. 'Does anyone up top know how that car came to topple over?'

'Someone took off the brakes,' Peter Key answered. 'It's Sam Soley's Old Reliable. He swears he meant to put a stone under the wheel, but forgot – he never had any car sense. He'd left the car facing the cliff where there's a one-in-ten slope. Someone only had to release the brakes and it would do the rest by itself. Someone didn't want a happy ending, did they?'

As he finished, a man wearing a thick blue jersey and a sailor's cap came up and said:

'You two had better come by boat, hadn't you?'

Roger felt an enormous relief.

'Good idea,' said young Key. 'Any more for the *Skylark*? Take it easy Superintendent. I'll lend you a hand.'

16

TWO DEAD, ONE ALIVE

THE LAUNCH took three-quarters of an hour to get to
Kemble, the nearest coast town with a hospital, and it was
nearly seven o'clock when Roger came out of a hot bath, put
on clothes provided by the local police, and felt reasonably fit
and able to cope. The ache across his back was the worst
consequence of his digging, but that only made him move
more slowly and more cautiously than usual. His head was
fairly clear, and on the launch and in the bath he had been
trying to assess the situation. Was Peter Key right, for instance,
and had someone released the brake of Sam Soley's car? Why
had the farmer left it pointing towards the cliff edge so danger-
ously? Why should anyone want to send the car crashing?
One thing was quite certain; anyone would have known that
it would follow the path of the MG, and if it had been done
deliberately, then it must have been in an effort to make sure
that something in the MG was destroyed – an effort ruthless
enough to risk the lives of at least three people.

Three?

An idea flashed into Roger's mind as he went into the office
of the Superintendent of the Kemble Police. Tenterden was
there, with the local chief, a big, burly man named Clark,
who kept in the background most of the time and seemed a
little over-awed by Roger.

'Glad you're looking so well,' Tenterden said, and there
was no doubt of his relief. 'I was afraid you'd had it, Handsome.'

'You weren't half as afraid as I was,' said Roger. 'How's
Salmon?'

Tenterden raised his hands, and let them fall.

'So he's gone,' said Roger heavily, and the news drove
the other thought out of his mind. 'How about the little fireman?'

'Dead when they dug him out.'

Roger felt depressed and heavy-hearted. Salmon had been
so keen, so game to go down those ropes, and but for the grace

of God he, Roger West, would have been that side of the MG. In fact, he had sent Salmon on to the side which had proved the fatal one.

Tenterden said: 'I've got a hell of a job on later, got to tell his wife.' He rubbed his thick neck. 'You suspect that second car was sent over deliberately, Handsome?'

'I've wondered.'

'I've questioned everyone who was there, and your chap Brown made sure I didn't miss anyone,' said Tenterden. For the first time, he smiled. 'When Brown realized what had happened and thought you were a goner, he would gladly have clapped everyone there into clink. Couldn't have been more upset if you'd been his blood brother. He's checking over every statement, looking for something which might help to find out who did it. The thing is, Soley left his driving-door window wide open – he always does. Hates a stuffy car, and likes to be able to put his hand inside and get things off the seat – like his pipe, or matches, or gloves.'

'Did anyone see him lean in today?'

'Yes – for some gloves,' Tenterden said. 'Anyhow, someone just had to pass the car, push an arm through that window, and release the hand-brake. We've got men down there working on it now, might pick up a print.'

Roger said. 'Yes. Who might have done it?'

'Soley himself obviously, either of the Key brothers, Mrs Richardson, Sydney Richardson, the three newspaper chaps, and two of our men,' said Tenterden. 'By cross-checking, we've managed to rule out everybody else we know. All the people I've mentioned passed between Soley's car and one next to it. Mrs Richardson and Sydney R. were together, the others were there one by one.'

'No one else on the list?'

'No one on the list, but there were several strangers about,' said Tenterden. 'The car was one of half a dozen dotted about there, and someone could have sneaked from one car to Soley's, then nipped back. Brown and my men will work all night to try to find out who else can go on the list, you needn't worry about that.'

'Thing that puzzles me,' began Clark, and then stopped and looked apologetically at Roger.

'Go on,' Roger urged.

'Don't want to interfere,' Clark said, 'but the thing that

110

puzzles me is why the car rolled over at all. I mean, it could have been an accident —'

'Try telling Brown that,' interpolated Tenterden.

'Got to face facts,' Clark said stubbornly. 'But if it wasn't an accident, why should anyone do it a-purpose?'

Tenterden didn't speak.

Roger said: 'How well do you chaps know the headland?'

'Pretty well,' answered Tenterden.

'Could anyone at the top be sure that the men carrying Rose Richardson had reached the sea?' asked Roger.

'Don't follow you,' said Clark.

'You mean, that everyone up top heard that she was alive and that someone might have made a desperate last-minute attempt to kill her and make sure she couldn't talk. That right?' Tenterden was eager.

'Yes.'

'Well I'm damned,' said Clark. 'Well, what's the answer, Art? If you ask me, no one could see that launch until it was some way out to sea. At the time the car went over it would only be fifty or sixty yards off shore. Could check the timing all right,' he went on, 'but you've got a point, Mr West.'

'I'll say he has,' said Tenterden. 'Couldn't see the reason for it before, but if someone had to make a last-minute attempt to kill Rose – my God, that'll be the answer!'

Roger said: 'Well, did it succeed?'

'Did what succeed?'

'The second attempt to kill her?' Roger asked, and felt almost absurd to put the question that way, instead of the direct: 'Is Rose Richardson alive or dead?' The weight of knowing that Salmon had gone was still heavy upon him.

Tenterden exclaimed: 'Didn't you know? She'll pull through, Handsome, that's one bit of good. They think she'll be able to tell us what happened this time tomorrow. I thought you knew.'

'No,' said Roger heavily, and he closed his eyes for a moment, then opened them widely and forced a smile. 'Well, that's fine. We'll need two men in her room until she's conscious, one man at the door, and one man at the window. If someone was so anxious to kill her that they'd let that car fall over the cliff, they won't stop at trying to kill her while she's in hospital. Have you —'

Tenterden jumped to his feet.

111

'You telephone the hospital, Clark,' he said. 'I'll go right over.'

'Right you are,' said Clark, but as he lifted the receiver he glanced at Tenterden and said: 'How about dinner? I warned the Cliff Hotel to have a table reserved for us, but they ought to know whether we're going.'

Tenterden looked at Roger.

'Like to eat here, or in Corby? It'll be an hour at least before we get to Corby, and — '

'Here.'

'I'll bring Mr West over to the hotel, and meet you there,' said Clark.

Young Peter Key and his brother Paul, who was ten years older, looked fifteen years older, and had all the signs of a heavy drinking, candle-at-both-ends life, were sitting in the dining-room of the Cliff Hotel, a large room with plush-seated chairs, huge crystal chandeliers, a curiously out-dated appearance of pomp and ceremony. All the waiters were in tails and white ties, the *maitre d'hôtel* was a little white-haired, white-bearded man, who obviously did not know whether to give preference to the Keys or to the police, and managed quite successfully to steer a half-way course.

They ordered soup, steaks, chips, and peas. A huge charcoal-broiled steak was put in front of Roger, enough for two or three meals. He did not feel as hungry as he might have done. He kept thinking of Salmon, of the way the Richardson girl had nearly died, and the freak chance which had saved her. He knew the folly of relying on a single witness for a vital statement, but there was a chance that she would be able to name whoever had attacked her. He found himself thinking of Richardson, too, and that wild rush to get over the edge of the cliff and down to his daughter. Richardson was the next man to talk to seriously, and the problem was to know exactly how to tackle the man. The velvet glove wasn't right, but the iron hand might be too rough. It wasn't easy to forget the struggle over Blake, and his own misgivings.

The Key brothers kept looking towards them. They were a course ahead of the police at the meal, and when Roger was pushing half of his steak away, Peter came over, his brother by his side. At closer quarters, Paul Key had an even more dissipated look, but his dark eyes were clear enough, and there

112

was an air about him, a kind of rakishness, as if he didn't give a damn for anyone else's opinion. The three policemen stood up, and Peter Key said:

'Don't get up, we're just off to Corby. Can't do anything more here, and Rose's out of danger. I just wanted to introduce my brother, Mr West.'

Roger said formally: 'How are you?'

'Always the better for meeting a hero,' said Paul Key, and there was a sardonic twist to his lips, a derisive glint in his eyes. 'My brother tells me that when everyone else would have jumped for safety, you stood by. Sorry the poor chap died in spite of it.'

'Yes. Most unfortunate,' Roger said, still stiffly.

'One word for it.' Paul had very white teeth and showed a lot of them when he smiled. 'How long will it be before you've put an end to this trouble, Superintendent?'

'Not long, I hope,' Roger said.

'May my friends and relations believe that, or are you simply being optimistic?'

Roger said: 'Supposing we wait and see what happens, Mr Key?'

Paul laughed.

'I know, I know, I'm asking far too many questions and you don't intend to be pumped. A man must always do his duty, mustn't he?'

'It will be a hell of a load off all our minds when we do know the truth of it,' said Peter Key. 'Mind if I ask you a straight question?'

'No.'

'Do you know how long someone's been trying to sabotage the works?'

'Have you any idea yourself?' asked Roger swiftly.

'No, but you—'

'Peter, you're wasting your time,' his brother said.

'Dry up, Paul,' said Peter. 'What I mean is, we had the guillotine trouble, and looking back we've had a lot more machine breakdowns lately than I can remember before. We put it down to a sequence of mishaps, but obviously it could be part of a pattern. Charlie Blake's never been so busy, and I expect you know just how many breakdowns there've been.'

'The paper-back binding machine, three stitching machines,

113

two of the flat-beds, one of the rotaries, five Monotype machines, and the new Linotype,' Roger said.

'Not bad,' said Paul. It was almost a jeer.

'Some of them might have been ordinary breakdowns, but some might have been fixed,' said Peter earnestly. 'No one's going to argue about the Monotype spools, that was deliberate damage. There's another thing which you may have missed, Mr West.'

'Never let it be thought,' jeered Paul.

Clark was looking annoyed. Tenterden seemed to know what to expect from the older Key, and Peter Key took it all so much for granted that obviously he was thoroughly used to his older brother's manner. He was still very earnest as he went on:

'I mean about Mr Richardson.'

'Eh?' asked Tenterden, as if startled.

'I think I know what Mr Key's getting at,' said Roger, 'and I half suggested it myself when I tried to make Richardson talk. The best way to sabotage the works would be to destroy the good relations which exist between the management and the workers. The easy way to spoil the relationship would be through Mr Richardson – by getting on his nerves, frightening him, and producing this near hysteria,' Roger said.

'Well, well,' murmured Paul Key. 'My brother has been saying almost that identical thing while we've been sitting at our table. Either this is a new kind of telepathy, or my estimation of politzia intelligentsia has been far too low.' The note in his voice was almost one of admiration. 'Yes. I have often wondered what would be the best way of bringing the old and ancient firm of Richardson and Key tumbling to its knees, so to speak —'

'Paul, dry up!' Peter interjected.

'Nonsense. I have decided that the proper thing is to give the police all the information within my power,' said Paul. 'I came to the conclusion that the lynch-pin of R. & K. was Sydney Richardson. My father keeps the sales up high and looks after the technical developments, and my faithful brother acts as a kind of liaison between customers and the works, oiling the wheels, so to speak, and making sure that deliveries are bang on the nail, but take Sydney R. away and the whole works would fall to pieces. My method would have been to murder Sydney R., but someone with a more subtle mind than

114

mine might have decided that it would be much more fun to let him watch everything breaking up. An exquisite refinement of torture. If I were in your position, Super, I would find out who enjoys watching Sydney R. writhing. Then you'll have your man, men, or women.'

17

STATEMENT

'I KNOW what I would do to that chap if I had my way,' said Clark gruffly. He watched the two brothers leaving the palatial dining-room, neither of them glancing round. From the back, they looked almost like father and son.

'How sour was Paul about getting out of the firm?' asked Roger.

Tenterden answered quietly: 'I couldn't be sure, Handsome, but I think it was a mutual arrangement. He was the chief sales representative at one time, and started playing the fool with buyers – and buyers' wives. He let himself be bribed into giving priority orders, and generally let the firm down. It came to a head when he persuaded the secretary of one of the customers to go off with him for a few weekends – she was a daughter of a director of the firm. They didn't get any more business from that source. Sir Lancelot Key went to find out why, and got the answer. So Paul was bought out.'

'How much would that mean to him?'

'I've heard rumours that the settlement was about a hundred and fifty thousand.'

'How long ago?'

'Four years.'

'So he should have plenty of money left.'

'No reason to think he hasn't,' answered Tenterden.

'Any reason to think that he hates the firm because he was thrown out?'

'No. He's the type who would find that a joke.'

Roger went on thoughtfully: 'But he would take inducements to give buyers the delivery they wanted in a big enough way to make it unethical.'

'That's as I understand it.'

'From whom?'

'Well, it's hard to say where these things come from,' said Tenterden, 'but there was a confidential secretary to Sydney Richardson – the girl who was doing most of the work that

116

Rose is doing now. This girl died. Natural causes – cancer – no need to think that it was the start of a chain of events,' went on Tenterden. 'She was a close friend of my wife.'

'Ah,' said Roger. 'What it is to be a native of Corby. Well, if Paul has that kind of unethical approach, if he was prepared to sell advantages in the trusted position he had, now that he's thrown out he might be open to take bribes from the firm's competitors, too.'

Tenterden looked very bleak.

'Well, I'll be damned,' said Clark.

'And as he knows the works so well, he could sell information about its most vulnerable workers and most vulnerable machines,' Roger went on. 'I think I'll telephone the Yard before we set out for Corby. I'll get them to make a closer check on Paul and his brother – on all the Keys, for that matter. Can I call from your office, Mr Clark?'

'You certainly can,' Clark said. 'As a matter of fact, Mr West, there's another thing you might think worth mentioning to Scotland Yard.'

'What's that?'

'I had two of my chaps out at Bracken Head,' volunteered Clark, and now he looked more uncertain of himself than ever. 'I was talking to one of them a while ago, and he said he saw a man named Tate at the Head while all the trouble was going on. He didn't see Tate do anything he shouldn't, mind you, but he's a man with a record.'

'Tate is?'

'Yes,' said Clark. 'You won't remember, Mr West, and there's no reason why you should, but we had some trouble at Kemble a year or two back. Race-course trouble. Some of the London race-course touts tried to shoulder the local people out, and there was a lot of ill-feeling. One or two men were badly hurt in a fight on the race-course, too. This Tate got six months for his part in it, and it wouldn't have been a miscarriage of justice if he'd had three years. He —'

Roger broke in softly: 'He worked with an older man, named Ragg.'

'So you do remember!'

'Ragg's employed at the R. & K. works,' Roger said, with rising tension. 'Tate isn't, but a man named Carter is. Tate, Ragg, and Carter made things too hot for themselves near the London race-courses, and worked the provinces for a few

117

years until you caught Tate. Is your man sure it was Tate at Bracken Head?'

'He ought to be,' said Clark simply. 'He arrested him. He's a little fellow, with a very small head and short dark hair. I don't know this Carter, I only heard about him.'

'We want to hear more about him,' Roger said grimly. 'I'll have the Yard send out for Tate and Carter and pick 'em up, too. We want to know if they've a small car, if they have some overshoes hidden away, where they were last night, and on the night of Jensen's murder.'

He lifted a telephone and put in a call to the Yard.

It was nearly ten o'clock when Roger and Tenterden entered Tenterden's office in Corby. There was a grim look about all of the policemen on duty, and it was obvious that the death of Salmon had struck them very hard. In the office, Brown was working with his coat off, his tie hanging loose, and a pile of cigarette stubs in an ashtray by his side. One of his eyes was watering, and there was a brown stain of nicotine at the left side of his lips.

'Better be born lucky than rich,' he greeted, and although his voice was rough, there was relief in his eyes. 'Got any other suicide attempts up your sleeves, Handsome?'

'Yes,' said Roger promptly. 'I want the handle of the hand-brake in Soley's car all in one piece, including any finger-prints on it.'

'Anyone up on that headland today would be wearing gloves. You haven't got an earthly,' Brown said. 'Anyhow, the steering-wheel, the brake and the gear lever, as well as the windscreen wiper switch, are all coming up. They've rigged up a conveyer system, and are working under flood lights. Lucky thing that car didn't fall below sea-level. What's this about wanting the Key family checked?'

'Who told you that?'

'I was talking to the Yard,' Brown said. 'Wanted more dope from Records about Ragg, Carter, and Tate – can't trace that car we're after, by the way. When I heard you'd been after the trio, I sent round to Ragg's digs. Lives at a house in Park Terrace. He's skipped, and the Yard says Carter and Tate have, too. Well, I talked to Scotty, asked him to put out a general call, and Scotty wanted to know what we were after the Keys for. It would be a help if I knew what was going on around here,' added Brown complainingly.

'Just keep your eyes and ears open, and one of these days you might be a detective!' Roger told Brown about Tate being at Bracken Head, and went on: 'If these three are our men they're doing the job for someone else, that's quite obvious. Paul Key might be our nigger-in-the-wood-pile, after all, if he's bearing a grudge. Arthur, there's another angle we haven't worked on enough: this might be a campaign against Richardson and Key, and it could also be a kind of personal vendetta, possibly against Sydney Richardson himself. We ought to find out who has cause to hate him – or who might have. Didn't you say that he wouldn't consent to Paul Key marrying Rose?'

'Yes.'

'Could that mean something?'

'I suppose so,' said Tenterden slowly. 'I shouldn't have thought – but oh, lor! I wouldn't have thought that any of this could have happened.' He eyed Roger broodingly and then went on: 'You've got someone in mind, haven't you?'

'I've got everyone in mind.'

'I know.'

'What's the history of the Farmer Soley and Sydney Richardson, or the Soley and Richardson and Key relationship?' inquired Roger.

Brown said: 'Soley?' as if he were thinking very hard.

'Just because Soley's car —' Tenterden began.

'It's much more than that,' Roger broke in. 'The girl's body was found in Soley's silo. Ever pause to think how difficult it would be to climb to the top of that silo carrying a dead body? A fireman could do it, or a steeplejack, a sailor, anyone used to climbing up iron ladders which rise almost perpendicularly, but no one else would find it easy – unless they were used to that particular silo.'

Tenterden didn't speak.

'Soley was on the spot as soon as we discovered the body,' Roger went on. 'And if the circumstantial evidence is right, Doris Blake was killed or at least attacked near the works gates, only a short distance from the back of Soley's Farm. Rose Richardson was attacked near the drive leading to the front of the farm. It's a kind of focal point. Add the fact that Soley's car was left in a position where it would be easy to fall over that particular piece of cliff, and it adds up to a lot of questions to ask Farmer Soley.'

'What the heck do I do with my mind?' Brown asked, almost humbly. 'That's all been in front of my nose, too.'

Tenterden stood up, pushed the hair back from his forehead, and smiled with his lips; his eyes still had the bleak look in them. It was a long time before he spoke, and then it was very slowly, ruminatively.

'I always knew that once things started to stir up in Corby the mud would get deeper and deeper, Handsome. And I knew I couldn't trust Arthur Tenterden to keep a detached point of view. I see everything from the Corby point of view. I get irritated when friends of mine are suspected of murder and violence. I know I shouldn't, but there it is – I don't like the idea of it at all. Browny wants to know what he does with his mind. I can tell you what I do with mine – I shut it tight, because I'm afraid of finding out a lot of things I don't want to find out. That's the truth about it, and if either of you find me covering up for anyone, for God's sake kick my pants off me.'

Roger was smiling, much easier in his mind than he had been since the news of Rose's disappearance. 'I will,' he promised.

'Now, about Soley and Richardson,' Tenterden went on, and frowned in concentration. 'Well, perhaps I'd better say Soley and the firm. He happened to clash with Richardson, but it was the firm which made the decision. It's nearly ten years ago, now.' Tenterden was looking very straight at Roger. 'The works wanted a new extension, and the obvious way was eastwards, into Soley's land. The Soleys have farmed that land for six generations, and Soley didn't want to part with it, so it had to be decided by the Corby Urban District Council. Everyone in Corby tried to get them to come to terms about it, but it wasn't any good. The works wanted the land, because in any other direction it would have meant building bridges, probably doing a lot of reclaiming, and always being in danger of floods. Soley said it was the richest part of his farm. Anyhow, the firm made a formal application to the Council, and of course the firm won. The firm always wins in Corby. It was referred to the Ministry, and the Council's order was confirmed. Soley gave way; he had to. They patched things up a bit, but they haven't been on the same good terms they used to be. All the same —'

He broke off.

'Motive one, Paul Key,' said Brown. 'Motive two, Sam Soley. What else have you got tucked away?'

'Handsome got on to that one earlier,' said Tenterden. 'Richardson and Key get a lot of big orders, and they're not the most popular firm in the trade. They've always stood out from the Federation of Master Printers, that's why Richardson hoped he could keep his men working. A lot of people in the trade dislike them, and would cash in if they were running at half cock. They've a very big output. This big export order for Bantu language text-books is worth half a million a year if they maintain delivery, and it's fabulous. Another firm might want it badly, so this could be some kind of business competitor, using either Paul or Soley or – no, dammit, I don't believe that!' Tenterden exclaimed, breaking off in mid-stream. His eyes flashed angrily. 'I just can't believe it.'

He broke off.

'When you feel like kicking yourself, you remember that the moment this job fell about your ears you got in touch with the Yard,' Roger said. 'You didn't even trust the county police to handle it, and you've got nothing to reproach yourself with. Coming with me?'

Tenterden looked startled.

'Where to?'

'First to see Soley, and then to see Richardson,' Roger said. 'Perhaps I ought to tackle Richardson on his own for a start.'

'I'll come with you to see Soley, anyhow,' Tenterden said slowly. 'What angle are you going to take?'

'Why did he release the brake of his car?' said Roger drily.

It was pitch dark when they passed the silo, but the lights at Soley's Farm showed up brightly; so Soley was still up. One of Tenterden's men was near the gate which led into the farm buildings, and reported that nothing unusual had happened. Roger and Tenterden approached the front door on foot, and Tenterden banged heavily on it. Almost at once footsteps sounded, and Sam Soley himself appeared. He looked a little odd, because he wore large horn-rimmed glasses. He glanced from one man to the other, and then said testily:

'Couldn't this wait until morning?'

'I'm sorry, Mr Soley, but we need to ask you one or two questions at once,' Roger said. 'May we come in?' They followed Soley into a big, untidy room, and it was easy to believe that Soley was a bachelor who did for himself. 'We needn't keep you long,' Roger added, and asked bluntly: 'Did you lean inside the door of your car and release the brake this afternoon?'

Soley pushed his glasses up over his forehead, and looked rather like an owl.

'Don't talk soft,' he said flatly. 'I didn't lean inside to release the brake, I wanted my gloves off the seat. Checked the brake was on, too; one of these days I'll lose my licence for forgetting it.'

Roger had a feeling that Tenterden was smiling.

'Did you see anyone near the car, or anyone touch it?'

Soley pulled the glasses down to the bridge of his nose, as if he was determined to make himself look peculiar.

'There was a little man, with a very small head. I know, because he drives a Ford Consul past my place most days. Don't ask me his name, because I don't think I've ever heard it. I'll point him out to you if I see him again.'

'Does he live near here?'

'Not as far as I know,' answered Soley, 'but I've known him give a man from the works a lift – meets him at the gates, sometimes. Chap who lives at Park Terrace.'

'Is this passenger small, dark-haired, and very thin?' asked Roger.

'That sounds like him,' Soley said.

'And it sounds like a man named Ragg, whom we're after,' Roger said. 'Thank you, Mr Soley. You understand that we have to check everything, don't you?'

'Why don't 'ee check the trouble at the works?' demanded Sam Soley, and opened the door for them to go.

'We want Ragg and his friends as fast as we can get 'em,' Roger said to Tenterden. 'Radio your HQ to ask the Yard to put on the pressure, will you? Then we'll get to work on Richardson.'

Tenterden was already switching on the radio.

'I quite understand why you should want to see my husband,' Mrs Richardson said, twenty minutes later, 'but I really can't allow it, Mr West. I would if I could, but he came straight home with me from Kemble, and he was in a state of absolute collapse, he really was. Dr Arnold gave him some sleeping tablets, and he only dropped off about half an hour ago. I simply can't let you wake him.'

She was in the drawing-room of the house not far from Soley's Farm, and Roger could not fail to notice the startling difference between the way this home was furnished and run, and Tenterden's home. Had it been the other way round, it would have been far less surprising. The room itself was pleasant and spacious, but the carpet was threadbare and the furniture mostly old-fashioned – inherited, Roger imagined, from the days when the firm of Richardson and Key had been less prosperous. A few old oil-paintings, of little value, were on the wall opposite the two large windows. Chintzes were pretty but inclined to be shabby. A photograph of an elderly man with a big white beard hung over the mantelshelf, looking down as if commandingly.

'This awful thing happening to Rose was almost too much for him,' said Mrs Richardson. She looked rather like the room, a little faded, obviously tired out and fighting for composure. 'I do hope you won't insist, Mr West. If you do, I shall have to ask Dr Arnold's permission, and I'm sure that he wouldn't readily grant it.'

'Mrs Richardson, do you know what's been worrying your husband so much?' demanded Roger.

'I only wish I did,' she said. 'I know it's something serious, and I can't think what it is except the strike. Can you come back in the morning? I just can't talk any more tonight. I'll make sure he doesn't get up until after lunch. If you come about eleven o'clock, say, I expect he'll be awake. I can't be sure that he will tell you anything, though.'

'Not even though he knows that his daughter is in such danger now?'

'I simply can't speak for him,' Mrs Richardson insisted. 'Sir Lancelot was here earlier this evening, he and my husband talked for a long time, so why don't you see if Sir Lancelot can help? He wouldn't stay any longer, he could see that the only thing for my husband was a good night's rest.'

Roger looked at her steadily, and said: 'Mrs Richardson, your daughter is still on the danger list. Your husband nearly died on the cliff. At least two people have been murdered. The firm of Richardson and Key is having a very difficult time, and might lose an order worth millions of pounds over a few years. The matter is desperately urgent, because we fear that the murderer or murderers might strike again. It's possible that your husband has some information which might help us to find out who it is. I want to see him now, please.'

Tight-lipped, Mrs Richardson looked at him defiantly; then she turned to a telephone near the door, lifted the receiver, and began to dial.

'I am calling Dr Arnold,' she said firmly. 'You – you can't go against a doctor's orders.'

Roger turned away, back towards her, and heard her cry out; there was a break in the dialling. He strode to the foot of the stairs, and then ran up them, his footsteps muffling all other sound. When he reached the top of the stairs he stopped to look round. He heard Mrs Richardson cry:

'Please hurry, doctor. Please hurry!'

Roger saw the open door of a big room, and the foot of a large bed. He looked inside. Nothing was going to make him soft-pedal with Richardson, the time had come when the man must be treated roughly – as roughly as Blake.

Then he saw the man, and stopped in his tracks, for Richardson was in bed, with only a sheet over him. He looked so still and stiff that he might be dead.

After the momentary shock, Roger swung round to the door, knowing that Richardson's condition might be desperate.

'Mrs Richardson!' he shouted. 'Your husband's ill! Get hot-water bottles, and more blankets, and don't lose a minute!'

He went to Richardson's side, felt his pulse and its faint beating, felt the cold flesh, saw the ashen cheeks, the eyes which were closed, the agonized expression. Then he saw an empty bottle, a piece of cotton-wool, a little white tablet on the floor by the bed. He pulled up the blankets, to start getting the man warm.

Soon he heard Mrs Richardson, rushing upstairs.

Then he heard a car outside.

18

PART OF THE TRUTH

ARNOLD TOOK one look at Richardson, and said: 'We need an ambulance, at once.' Then he looked at the empty bottle, and said: 'You can tell the hospital to get ready for a case of acute barbiturate poisoning.'

Mrs Richardson was thrusting hot-water bottles beneath the blankets, and muttering as she did so. Roger went downstairs, picked up the telephone, and dialled.

The ringing sound stopped, and a man said in a deep, leisurely voice:

'Corby Police Station.'

'This is Superintendent West,' Roger said briskly.

'Oh, yes, sir!'

'First arrange for an ambulance to come to Mr Sydney Richardson's house. Then brief the hospital that a case of an overdose of barbiturate will be in very soon. Dr Arnold is in charge. Then ask Mr Tenterden and Mr Brown to ring me at Mr Richardson's house. All clear?'

'I've got all that, sir,' the man said, his voice still deep but not hurried.

Roger rang off.

He heard Mrs Richardson ask: 'How bad is it, doctor?'

'I don't know yet,' answered Arnold, his voice softer with understanding and sympathy. 'I expect we shall be able to pull him round, though.'

Roger started up the stairs.

'Poor darling,' Mrs Richardson said in a steady voice. 'What a dreadful, dreadful time he's having. Do you think he— ?' She broke off, Roger reached the landing behind her, and she went on as if to herself: 'He always said he couldn't stand it any longer, that he would kill himself if it didn't stop.'

'Mary —' Arnold began.

'If what didn't stop?' demanded Roger.

Arnold was at the foot of the bed in a room which was immediately over the big room downstairs. All Roger could see of it now was the big wardrobe on the wall at one side, two chairs, a part of a gilt mirror, and the foot of the bed itself, with Richardson's feet making a hillock beneath the bed-clothes. Mrs Richardson was just inside the room, and she started when Roger called out. The doctor looked as if he were going to protest. He actually opened his mouth; it was hard to imagine a more insignificant little man, with his smalmed down hair and smooth face and rather small eyes and thin lips. He didn't speak, after all. Mrs Richardson put her hands to her face, and stood quite still.

'It's time you told us everything you know, Mrs Richardson,' Roger said. 'If you keep anything back, you might be responsible for anything else that happens.'

Arnold closed his mouth and pursed his lips, then said unexpectedly and quickly:

'Mary, Mr West is quite right. It is your duty to tell him everything you can. It may help Sydney. It may help Rose. You mustn't keep anything else back. Tell him all you can, there's a good woman.' It was almost as if he meant to say: 'There's a good girl.'

Not far off, a car engine sounded as Mrs Richardson turned round slowly, looked at Roger, and said in a low-pitched, pain-racked voice:

'Ever since the strike he's been getting threatening letters, that's the truth. Ever since the strike someone's been saying they would ruin the works. He told me not to say anything, he made me promise. He – he said that it was a matter he had to work out for himself.' All the colour was drained from her face, and her eyes seemed almost colourless too. 'He was almost beside himself, about a year ago, and I made him tell me. He pretended he wasn't really worried, only angry, because it was some madman who had a grudge against him, but I could see that he was getting more and more distressed. That – that's why I asked Rose to go and work at the works. I thought she might be able to find out more, she might be able to help him. He was always so fond of Rose.' She spoke almost as if she was thinking of her husband in the past. 'Sometimes I would try to make him talk about it, but he told me that I mustn't tell anyone else, that it would be all right, that I wasn't to question him about it. And – and I didn't. I just couldn't.'

There was the sound of another engine, this time louder, and it was drawing nearer; this would be the ambulance.

Roger hoped that the telephone bell wouldn't ring just yet, he wanted more time to talk to the woman.

'How many letters have there been?' he said.

'I don't know, I only know about three or four.'

'Have you got one now?'

'No. Syd – Syd wouldn't let me see them.'

'Do you know if he kept them?'

'He burned some of them, I know,' answered Mrs Richardson wearily. 'I don't think he kept them. I – I used to search for them, and I expect he realized that. It – it wasn't only letters, though. Sometimes he would get telephone calls, I believe he had them even when he went to London. I watched him getting worse and worse, in front of my eyes, and there wasn't anything I could do to help him, there just wasn't a thing.'

The car, or ambulance, was just outside.

Arnold said: 'I'll go and open the door.' The man had a genius for doing the right thing, and he pushed past Mrs Richardson and then past Roger, while the woman was closing her eyes, and tears seemed to be squeezing between the lids.

'Why didn't you tell Dr Arnold, or Sir Lancelot, or even Superintendent Tenterden?' Roger asked quietly.

'Syd told me not to,' she whispered, 'and I daren't disobey him. If I'd disobeyed him, he wouldn't have had anyone to help him. He used to come home from the works sometimes absolutely done in, and if I'd nagged at him, or if he'd thought he couldn't trust me, it would have been the last straw. I just had to do what he said.' She caught her breath, screwed up her eyes tightly, and said in a shrill voice: 'It's a wife's duty to do what her husband wants.'

There were voices downstairs, and Arnold said: 'Good, you were very quick. It's Mr Richardson. Upstairs.' He led the way, and Mrs Richardson went into the room, Roger followed her, and saw the unconscious man again. He was lying with blankets piled over him, his face ashen grey, and his lips bloodless. His eyes looked huge, although they were closed, the eyeballs pressing darkly against the almost translucent lids. He looked an old man near to death; or an old man who had been taken in death, for there was no movement at his lips or at his chest as far as Roger could detect.

On a table by his side was the small, empty bottle. The piece of cotton-wool was by it, and a glass partly filled with water.

The screw cap of the bottle was on the floor by the side of the table. Roger went towards it, and studied the unconscious man and wondered whether there was any hope at all for him.

Arnold and the ambulance men came in.

'I must come with him,' Mrs Richardson said. Roger expected Arnold to say that she mustn't go, but should have some rest; instead, the doctor simply said:

'Get a hat and coat then, Mary, and when we've made Sydney comfortable, you must come and stay with us.' He superintended the removal of Sydney Richardson, the two white-smocked ambulance men looking like pall bearers. He hovered about Mrs Richardson as she took a small cloth hat and a brown tweed coat from the wardrobe, helped her on with the coat, and then went downstairs with her. Roger followed them closely, seeing car headlamps on the road at the foot of the drive. He guessed that Tenterden had come instead of telephoning. Mrs Richardson was in Dr Arnold's car when Roger called:

'Dr Arnold, can you spare me a moment?'

The ambulance doors were closing on Richardson.

'It mustn't be more than a moment,' Arnold said, and came forward briskly.

'I know, and I appreciate your co-operation very much indeed,' Roger said. 'Just one question: how was it that Richardson had access to so many tablets?'

'We don't know yet how many he took,' said Arnold, 'but he has been taking sleeping tablets for a long time. For twelve months, at least. It would be quite easy to accumulate enough to kill himself, and — ' He hesitated, and in the light from the hall and the headlamps, he looked very grave. 'It will be my duty, if I am called, to say that Mr Richardson has threatened to take his own life on several occasions. That is the sad truth. It is quite possible that he anticipated this day by accumulating the tablets. I did all I reasonably could, Mr West. I had his wife watch him carefully, and report all his movements and moods. She has had a terrible time, a terrible time.'

'I can imagine,' Roger said. 'Did you know about these threats?'

'I only knew that Richardson was in great distress, but had no idea what caused it,' said Dr Arnold. 'He simply would not talk. Now, I must go.' He saw the ambulance moving slowly

128

down the drive, turned to his own car as Tenterden and
Brown, two huge figures, got out of the car which had just
arrived. 'Good evening, Arthur,' he said to Tenterden.

'How bad is it?' asked Tenterden.

Arnold glanced swiftly at the car, as if trying to judge
whether Mrs Richardson would hear anything that was said,
lowered his voice, and answered:

'Not good. Very little chance. I'll see you later.'

Then he climbed into his car, and jabbed the self-starter.

19

SEARCH

'I SUPPOSE it was inevitable,' Tenterden said glumly. 'And I suppose I ought to have anticipated it and made sure it couldn't happen. I just didn't know that the Richardsons would be on their own tonight. I thought Sir Lancelot and one of the sons would be there, there's plenty of room.' He sounded as if he hated himself and hated the world. 'Arnold wouldn't talk like that unless he thought Syd was a goner.'

'He could be wrong,' Roger said briskly. His eyes were stinging with tiredness, and after the excitement he was acutely conscious of his aching back, but there could be no rest for several hours. 'Heard anything from Bracken Head yet?'

'Had a message just before we left,' answered Tenterden. 'They've got the Austin free of the MG, so they can get inside it. They won't get at that hand-brake or the steering-wheel much before morning, but there won't be another fall of cliff to bury the car or send it down into the sea. That's the main thing.'

'Yes,' Roger said. 'Something, anyhow. Arthur, who hates Richardson enough to do this?' He told the story of the threatening letters and the telephone calls, watching the Corby man's expression all the time.

They were in the hall of Richardson's house, where all the lights were on. The ambulance and Arnold's car had long been out of sight and earshot.

'Mrs Richardson says it started about the time of the strike, but I'm beginning to doubt the importance of the strike,' Roger went on. 'Richardson didn't make any open enemies, did he?'

'No,' rumbled Tenterden. 'More likely he hated some individuals. He had reason to hate the guts of the men who wouldn't stay in work and wouldn't try to stop the others coming out.'

'This worsening of the management-and-worker relationship – it's been gradual, and due chiefly to Richardson's temper, hasn't it?'

130

'As far as I know.'

'No groups or factions in the works would hate Richardson enough to work on him like this?' When Tenterden didn't answer, Roger went on: 'It doesn't stand to reason. These chaps work there. It's one thing to strike for better conditions and wages, but no one in his senses would want to break the firm, certainly not anyone in Corby. They would be killing their own livelihood. So we're back to some competitor, or to a personal motive against Richardson.'

'I know,' Tenterden said.

'And the more I think about it, the less likely it seems that this is from competition,' Roger went on. 'The sabotage could be due to someone being paid by a rival firm who would like to get the big Bantu order, I suppose, but that looks too obvious. The whole job has an inside look to me, in spite of the men who broke in and killed Jensen. Until we've some evidence that a competitive firm is behind it I think we can soft-pedal on that angle.'

Tenterden was very subdued, obviously because of what had happened to Richardson. He looked tired, too, and more dispirited than Roger had seen him.

'Anything in from London about the Keys or the Ragg mob?' asked Roger.

'Nothing that helps us yet,' answered Brown. 'The Yard's put the call out everywhere – they'll be picked up soon.' He stifled a yawn. 'Oughtn't we to get some more chaps out to turn this place upside down now we've the chance?'

'No,' said Roger, and glanced at Tenterden. 'We don't want a lot of Corby coppers going over the place, do we? This is our job.'

'Gawd,' breathed Brown.

'I think you're wise,' said Tenterden, brightening. 'I'll work all night if necessary.'

'If Handsome works all night he'll be flat out tomorrow when we need him most,' said Brown grumbling, 'but I suppose we'll have to do it his way. What do we want to check, Handsome?'

'That bottle the tablets were in and the glass by it, for prints,' Roger said. 'Then we want a search of the whole house for threatening letters or for anything which might give us an idea who hates Richardson.' He didn't repeat that he was beginning to feel certain that this was a case of a personal

131

vendetta against Sydney Richardson; he wouldn't say so until he could see how the murder of Jensen and Doris fitted in. He realized that so much had happened during the day that he had almost forgotten the engineering foreman who was on remand in Colchester; the case seemed to have gone far beyond the original murders, and its implications were so much deeper.

And Blake might hate Richardson . . .

Roger rejected that, sharply. Whoever hated Richardson had kidnapped his daughter and nearly killed her; had sent Soley's car hurtling over the cliff; and had taken Richardson to the verge of death. It couldn't be Blake; in fact, there was a good case for believing that Blake should never have been charged.

'Where do we start?' inquired Brown.

'Richardson's got a small office here, where he works at weekends and in the evenings.' Tenterden said. 'There's a safe, too. We'll start in there.'

They worked solidly for a little over two hours. Roger's eyes felt as if they had sandpaper behind them, and he kept straightening up to rest his back, but he felt more determined than ever to finish the search. Once he had accepted its inevitability, Brown worked with a will, and Tenterden with a thoroughness which Roger had come to expect from him. But they found nothing about theatening letters, little about business, nothing at all to help them. The safe, an old-fashioned kind, had not been locked, and obviously it was used against fire rather than against burglars. There were bundles of securities, both in Richardson's name and his wife's, and details of other securities lodged in the bank for safe keeping; and there were some of Rose Richardson's securities, too. None of the family was poor. Rose had nearly ten thousand pounds in her own right, and some shares in Richardson and Key. Richardson himself was worth over fifty thousand, his wife at least thirty thousand pounds. Each had made a will, and each had left a third of the estate to Rose, and two-thirds to husband or wife. All this was quite normal. Roger glanced through the wills and the securities, pondered over the figures, and tried to square what he knew of Sydney Richardson with everything that this implied.

Then he came upon Richardson's bank statements, and found heavy withdrawals of cash over the past three months – a total of over two thousand pounds more than average.

'Know what that could mean, don't you?' Tenterden said heavily. 'That he's been blackmailed, too.'

'Could be,' conceded Roger non-committally.

'If it was blackmail the blackmailer didn't bleed him enough to do him any harm financially,' Brown said thoughtfully.

Certainly Richardson had no financial anxieties of any kind, Roger mused. Richardson and Key as a firm was flourishing more than ever, in spite of the troubles at the works, none of which had been more than a pin prick – although the cumulative effect might be considerable over a period, and there might be worse to follow.

'Who'd hate the man enough to do this to him?' Brown asked heavily.

Roger didn't speak.

'Can't even be sure he'll come round enough to make a statement,' Brown went on. 'This is as tough a one as I've come up against, I will say that.'

It was a little before three o'clock when Tenterden stood back from a writing bureau in Rose Richardson's bedroom, yawned, and said:

'Well, that's the lot, and we haven't proved a thing.'

'Not a sausage,' Brown said, with gloomy satisfaction; he just saved himself from adding: 'I told you so.'

'We know he's paid out two thousand pounds in cash recently,' Roger said. 'That could have been to Ragg and his friends, if they're involved. How about watching this place, Arthur?' he asked abruptly.

'I'll send for some of my chaps to guard the place back and front,' answered Tenterden. 'Got six on duty at the works. I'll need some more help if this goes on much longer.' He telephoned his office, gave instructions, and then went on: 'Now we'll go to my place for a cup of tea and a snack. After that I think you ought to do what Browny tells you, Handsome – put your head down for a few hours.'

'That's all right with me,' Roger said. 'Ask the station to check on Rose Richardson's condition, will you?'

When they reached Corby they were told that Rose Richardson was out of danger, that her father was still in a coma and Dr Arnold had little hope of his recovering, and that Mrs Richardson was at the doctor's home. Ten minutes afterwards, they went to Tenterden's house. Roger was surprised to find the lights on, and Mrs Tenterden in a red silk dressing-gown, high at the neck, was at the door to greet them. Tea and sandwiches were ready in the spotless modern kitchen. Tenterden's wife looked bright-eyed, and nothing like as tired as the men.

'Mrs Arnold called and told me about Mary Richardson, and I went round to see her,' she said. 'I've only been back for an hour.' She was perched on a kitchen stool while the men were seated round the small table with its blue Formica top, demolishing the sandwiches. 'I know that a policeman's wife should be seen and not heard, but haven't you any idea who's responsible for all of this yet?'

'No, Maggie,' Tenterden said, and summoned a smile. 'Now tell us who it is?'

Maggie Tenterden smiled back, a little mockingly. Roger saw Brown eyeing her with admiration, and felt the same kind of admiration himself. Although she had expected all three men, she had cleaned her face of make-up, and it was shiny with some kind of night cream. Her thick hair was in a red net, and pulled back from her forehead, her temples and the back of her neck.

'I know where I would look, dear,' she said, and glanced up out of the window, smiling faintly and giving the impression that she was really saying: 'See where I'm looking.' Roger was jolted out of his tiredness, and he watched first the woman and then Tenterden, who was frowning as if wishing that his wife would not behave like this.

'Where?' demanded Brown bluntly.

'I think Sam Soley has more hate in his little finger than everyone else in Corby put together,' Maggie said. 'Don't say I haven't warned you, Art, I have several times. He's never forgiven the firm for taking that land from him, and if you ask me, it's turned his mind. Of course no one will take any notice of me, but you mark my words.' She was nursing her knees, and held her head back; when she finished she smiled broadly.

'You're not so smart,' her husband said disparagingly. 'You've worked that out after living here for thirty years. Handsome thought of Soley after being here for about four days. But you're both guessing, and —'

The telephone bell rang.

He said. 'Who the blasted —?' and then broke off. His wife

134

stretched out her right hand and picked up a red telephone standing on a small shelf bracketed to the wall. She held it out to Tenterden as he got up. 'Tenterden here,' he grunted. 'Who . . . what?' He closed his eyes for a moment, not from tiredness but because he was suffering from some new kind of shock, and it seemed a long time before he said: 'All right, ta . . . No, it's all right.' He put down the receiver, pushed his fingers through his hair, and announced in a steady voice: 'Richardson's gone.'

Brown exclaimed: 'Dead?'

Tenterden nodded glumly.

'Oh, poor Mary,' Maggie Tenterden exclaimed, and her smile vanished.

Roger said slowly: 'So we're back even farther than when we started.' He rubbed his eyes as he stood up from the table. 'Mrs Tenterden — '

'My men friends call me Maggie,' Mrs Tenterden said, but it was a strangely pathetic attempt to be flippant, and the hurt was still in her eyes. 'Yes?'

'Why did you name Soley?'

'Surely I told you,' she said.

'You told us of his hate, you didn't say why you should be so sure.'

'Call it feminine intuition,' Maggie said, and then she moved towards Roger and touched the back of his hand. 'Don't take any notice of me. I suppose it *is* intuition, but I haven't any real reason for saying it's Sam Soley, except that – well, I've never liked our Sam. I think he's a nasty little man. When he was young, if he couldn't get everything he wanted he used to have to hit someone, hurt someone badly. Isn't that true, Art?'

'You always have exaggerated,' Tenterden said, and then shrugged his shoulders. 'Oh, it's true up to a point, but there's no reason at all to suspect Soley. All the same — ' He broke off. 'Think we ought to have an eye kept on him, Handsome?'

'It was his car that nearly buried you alive,' said Brown.

'And killed Tom Salmon,' Maggie put in.

'We'll sift every piece of evidence in the morning and decide whether to tackle him then,' said Roger. 'Soley isn't likely to run away. We haven't heard if there were any finger-prints on that bottle from which Richardson took the tablets,' he added.

'Oh,' said Tenterden. 'Sorry. The station just told me. Only Richardson's.' He pushed his fingers through his hair again,

135

and went on: 'Well, we'll soon know whether it's a personal feud. If the trouble stops now Richardson's dead there'll be some reason to think so. But if it doesn't —'

He broke off.

Roger said: 'I'm going round to the hotel, I want to see the Keys fairly early in the morning, and I'd better be able to talk sense.' He turned towards the door.

'We've a spare room with twin beds, and the beds are made and ready for you and Browny,' said Maggie Tenterden. 'That way you'll get a longer night's sleep and a better breakfast — provided you don't mind being the guest of a country copper.'

'You try to keep me away from that bed,' Brown said, and his face lit up, but that was the only moment of relief from gloom.

20

NOT OVER YET

ROGER WAS aware of subdued noises, of bright light on his eyes, of a heavy head, of repugnance to the very idea of waking. Then the voices became more insistent, they were a man's and a woman's, and he recognized Maggie Tenterden's. He forced himself to open his eyes. He was on the bed nearer the door in the pleasant, white-painted room where Tenterden had shown him the previous night; Brown had the bed closer to the wall, and was still asleep; at least, he was lying still. Roger eased himself up on his pillows, and Maggie Tenterden, wearing a short-sleeved dress which fitted her slim figure like a sheath, her hair done, her make-up beautiful, stood in the doorway holding a tea-try. Behind her was Dr Arnold, behind him a taller man from the Corby Police Station. There was a sense of emergency about the whole visitation.

Roger sat up.

'Good morning,' Maggie greeted. 'I tried to keep them at bay until you'd had time to wake, but they wouldn't listen, and Arthur's in the bath.' She put the tea-tray down on the side table at Roger's bed, looked across at Brown, and added laughingly: 'There's a man who really knows how to sleep.'

Brown was making a noise between a grunt and a snore.

'Thanks,' said Roger gratefully, and noticed her long, slender hands as she poured out a cup of tea. 'What's new, Doctor?'

Arnold said: 'I think you should know at once that the poison which killed Richardson was exclusively barbiturate, the drug in all the sleeping tablets which I prescribed for him. There was no additional factor.'

Roger sipped tea.

'How many did he take?'

'Very difficult to say, except in certain circumstances,' replied Arnold. 'Perhaps fifteen. I wanted to report to Superintendent Tenterden, but I have several urgent calls to make, so I must ask you to pass on this message.' There wasn't a vestige of humour in the little man. He backed away. 'No doubt I shall see you later. The official post-mortem report should be prepared by midday.' He reached the door, and added: 'Rose Richardson is conscious and will be able to make a statement during the morning.'

He vanished past the Corby plain-clothes man, and Maggie walked after him; Roger heard her talking as they went downstairs. The Corby man, not unlike Salmon to look at but younger and fuller in the face, stood in the doorway as if diffidently, as Roger asked:

'And what have you got for us?'

'A report from Superintendent Clark of Kemble, sir,' the man said, and came forward with a sealed envelope. 'I was instructed to hand it to you or to Mr Tenterden in person. I'm sorry to have arrived at such an inconvenient hour.'

'It's all right,' Roger said, and took the report, slit the envelope open with the handle of a teaspoon, and took out several folded sheets of paper, each filled with small-face typewriting. 'Arrange for Mr Tenterden and me to see Miss Richardson at the hospital in an hour's time,' went on Roger, and in the same breath asked: 'Does Mrs Richardson know what happened last night?'

'I believe Dr Arnold broke the news to her, sir.'

'Good,' said Roger, and hitched himself up on his pillows and began to read the report, a model in presentation, and a pleasure to read. He looked for the entry opposite *Handbrake,* and read:

Hand-brake. Pistol type, released by pressure of forefinger. Chromium and cellulose in good condition. Trigger well worn and polished. Only prints: Mr S. Soley's. Prints checked against other articles known to be handled by Mr Soley. Some sign of smearing through use of glove. Main prints show top and middle joint of right hand, could be commensurate with pressure exerted from the doorway by person leaning in at open door or window.

Roger read this again, his heart beginning to thump.

'What've you got?' asked Brown, and Roger turned to see him half-way up in bed, hair standing on end, face looking grubby and unshaven, eyes bleary.

Roger said: 'The indications are that Soley handled the brake of that Austin just before it ran down the cliff.'

'Who's surprised?' asked Brown, and looked towards the door. 'What a woman! You wouldn't think Arthur T. would

138

have anything to attract her, would you? Don't mind admitting I pretended to be asleep, I am not a thing of beauty first thing in the morning. Got a spot of tea?'

Roger passed him the tray.

'Ta,' said Brown. 'Well, it's a case of the obvious again, isn't it? Everything pointed to Soley, and now this does. What's it say?' He listened as Roger read it out, and then went on: 'That chap Clark seems good. I did a hand-brake print check last month, remember that case where we thought the man had fiddled with the brake to send his wife down Putney Hill? We proved he would have made the print on one side if he'd leaned in the car and done it, the brake had been released by direct pressure from someone sitting in the driving-seat. This is the reverse. On the strength of that we've got a lot to say to Soley.'

'After we've talked to Rose Richardson,' Roger said. 'I wonder if she knows about her father.'

The moment he stepped into the hospital ward, he felt sure that Rose knew about Richardson. That showed in the shadows in her eyes, in the tension at her lips, which were still red and puffy from the adhesive plaster. Apart from that and some bruises on her cheek and at her wrists, she looked fairly normal.

Tenterden was with Roger, and he said:

'We can't tell you how sorry we are about your father, Miss Rose, and we hate having to worry you, but we can't avoid it.'

'I know,' said Rose; her voice was hoarse and tired.

'We'll make it as quick as we can,' Roger promised her, and he already had a mental note of what he wanted to ask. 'How many men attacked you?'

'Two,' she said.

'Did you recognize either of them?'

'No, unfortunately.'

'Did you notice anything about them which might help us to identify them?'

'I think they were young, and each was quite small,' Rose answered. 'One man was very thin. I can remember every moment of what happened vividly. I've been thinking about it a great deal, especially since I heard what happened to my father.' There was no venom in her voice, but a hardness which told its own story: she wanted above everything else to help them catch the attackers. She told them exactly what had happened, even to the moment when one car drew alongside and there had been an exchange of shouts. She remembered exactly what had been said, and Tenterden made notes. Each man felt her horror, each hated the men who had talked so cold-bloodedly about killing her, in her hearing.

'Did they give the slightest hint about this man who laid the golden eggs?' Roger asked.

'Absolutely none.'

'And you can't place either of the voices?'

'No,' she answered, 'although I think I could recognize one of them if I heard it again. The noise of the engine drowned the other.' She hesitated, and then went on rather more slowly, as if she wasn't quite sure of herself: 'I recognized one thing, though.'

Tenterden exclaimed: 'Ah!'

'What was it?' asked Roger.

'The car which drew alongside,' answered Rose flatly. 'It was Sam Soley's old Austin. I recognized the mascot in front, a big fish. I don't think it was Sam at the wheel, but I can't really be sure,' she added. 'There was the roar of the engines and the wind was cutting in at the window. It might have been Sam, but I couldn't swear to it. I can swear to the car.'

'That's very helpful, Miss Richardson,' Roger said. 'Is there anything else to help us?'

'I don't think so.'

'Did you know that your father was being threatened, and getting poison-pen letters and telephone calls?'

'I didn't know, although I was afraid it was something like that,' answered Rose. 'I did everything I could to find out what was worrying him, and yesterday and the day before I questioned all the foremen and department managers. I've been lying here and wondering whether that was why they attacked me.'

'You mean, whether any one of them thought you had made some discovery which might incriminate him.'

'I hadn't thought of it as formally as that, but I suppose that's what it amounts to,' Rose answered. 'I've been going over everything I said and everyone I talked to, and I can't think of anything that will help.'

'What we would like you to do is make a list of all the men

140

you discussed this with, and as far as possible, a note of exactly what you said to them,' Roger urged. 'Also whether they answered freely, or showed any sign of resentment at being questioned. Can you do that?'

'Yes,' she answered, 'but not for some time. I arranged with Paul Key to come and fetch me and take me home this afternoon.'

'This evening will be fine,' Roger said briskly. 'Will Sir Lancelot be at home with you?'

'Yes,' Rose answered. 'I don't feel that I can be there alone with mother, after this – not for a few days, anyhow. Peter and Paul will be staying, too. If they had stayed last night—' She broke off, screwing up her eyes. In that moment she was remarkably like her mother, although Roger had never noticed the similarity before. 'If there is anything at all I can do, please let me know.'

'Believe me we will,' promised Roger.

When he left, he was reminding himself that it had been almost as if he had been fated not to talk freely to Richardson before the man died, and the same kind of frustrating situation was building up with the Keys. He had hardly talked to them except at the hotel with Paul, and a few minutes with Peter Key when the younger member of the family had behaved so coolly and capably; he was a youth quite used to making quick decisions, and there was a kind of cold-bloodedness about him which should not be overlooked. Now, however, Roger wanted to get back to Corby and talk to Soley again; and the Keys were coming to collect Rose.

The Keys would have to wait ... One law for the rich?

What the hell was the matter with him? If he'd half the suspicions of the Keys that he had had of Blake, he would have had them here days ago. So Soley was next.

He changed his mind abruptly. Tenterden was having the farmhouse and the whole of the farm watched, and nothing about that need surprise Soley. There was the risk that some policeman friend of the farmer's would let fall a word of warning or careless hint, but in any case Soley was too conspicuous a figure to get far without being noticed. All the roads leading from Corby were blocked, and there was a policeman on duty at the bus station and the railway station.

'I'll wait here and talk to the Keys,' Roger said to Tenterden. 'Would you rather get back to Corby?'

141

'Much rather stay with you on this session,' Tenterden said. It was then a quarter to one. 'What did you think of Rose?'

'I got a feeling that she suspects more than she'll say,' Roger told him, 'but I haven't any reason for thinking so. Everyone in Corby from your wife downwards knows more about the background to this case than I do. I wish —'

He broke off as Superintendent Clark drove into the hospital courtyard at a faster speed than he should have, jammed on the brake, got out and slammed the door, and contrived to give the impression of haste as well as emergency. Roger felt his nerves tautening as the man came striding towards him.

'Just had a message from your office,' he said to Tenterden. 'There's some trouble at Richardson and Key's – that big order they were so worried about is all mucked up. I don't know the rights of it, something to do with formes tampered with during the night. Sir Lancelot Key telephoned. He's staying on the spot, with his sons, and he wants us to take Miss Richardson back to Corby. Like me to look after that while you get back to the works?'

'We can't get there soon enough,' Roger said.

The journey took them forty minutes, for Tenterden could drive as fast as young Tom Cousins. They passed the van as they headed for the works gates, a little after two o'clock. Gordon the gatekeeper saluted them as they went by, and two Corby plain-clothes men were on duty at the gates. No one was about outside, and when Roger stepped into the works itself he was aware of a strange quiet, as if all the machines had stopped working. He saw Paul Key coming across the works yard, that sardonic smile curving his lips, and as he drew up he said:

'I'm to take you to the scene of the latest crime, gentlemen. And although I say it myself, this one really is a beaut.'

Tenterden spoke with unexpected sharpness.

'Do you really think that anything about this affair is a joking matter, Mr. Key?'

Paul looked surprised, drew in his breath as if to rasp a reply, then shrugged his shoulders and led them, stalking, towards the room beyond the Casting Room, the huge building with the countless tables, or stones, in it, each laden with the type formes locked ready for printing. The double doors leading to the Flat-bed Machine Room were open, and beyond these were several tables, and round one of the tables a group of men, including Sir Lancelot Key and his son Peter.

Not a single machine was running; the works of Richardson and Key had been brought to a standstill.

21

STANDSTILL

SIR LANCELOT KEY stood by one of the big tables, one
hand leaning against it, head raised, in a pose which had a kind
of considered artiness. He was slightly shorter than Peter,
whose eyes seemed to glitter, and who was clenching his right
fist. Explosively, he said:

'That's cost us millions. Millions! My God, it's time we put
an end to this.'

'Hear, hear,' said Paul, only just loud enough for Roger to
hear.

'Exactly what has happened?' asked Roger, going forward
a step ahead of Tenterden and Brown.

Sir Lancelot looked round at him, drew up to his full height,
and in a curious way reminded Roger of Richardson; it was
as if this man had also been driven to the limits of his endur-
ance, and was controlling himself only by a great effort.

Peter rapped: 'I thought the works was supposed to be
watched and guarded.'

'No unauthorized person has been in or out,' Roger said as
roughly.

'Next thing you know you'll be saying that this is our
imagination,' said Peter. His hands were still clenched tightly,
he looked as if he would like to shriek out at someone handy,
and the handiest person was Roger. 'Well, it isn't imagination.
We shall lose the biggest single order that this company has
ever received, a five-year contract for — ' He broke off, splut-
tering, and Roger was amazed at the change in him. Physical
danger hadn't affected him the other day, but mental stress
knocked him to pieces.

'Just how was it done?' asked Roger quietly.

'I don't see that — '

'We must co-operate with the police, Peter,' Sir Lancelot
said heavily. 'All the doors were locked, remember, and a
constant police patrol was kept on the outside of the works.
No one was allowed inside. And yet during the night — ' He

broke off, drew a deep breath, and then swung round towards a small pile of folded sheets, and a thinner pile of flat sheets. He opened a book at random, and thrust it in front of Roger's nose. 'Now do you understand?'

Roger looked down, and a moment or two were enough to tell him what had happened; words had been misspelt, sentences had been altered, to make nonsense. He turned to another page; here the alterations and absurdities in the text were fewer, but were still considerable. He flipped through several pages, and most of them had some spoiled words.

'How was it done?' he demanded.

'Why the hell didn't the Yard send someone who knew a bit about printing?' Peter Key demanded.

'This is how it happened,' said his father, and turned and pushed past the little group of workmen gathered near, led Roger through into the room where all the bigger machines stood in their long rows. Again, that unnatural silence, silence as of the night, pervaded everything. Men and women, at a ratio of about three to one, were standing or sitting about idly. In one corner two girls and a man were giggling, but they stopped abruptly. In another several men were squatting on boxes, and playing cards. Everyone turned round when they saw the Keys and the police enter. Sir Lancelot went to one of the big machines, where three men were standing.

'This is where the sabotage was discovered,' he announced. 'These men noticed it when reading some of the freshly printed sheets. You understand enough about the work to know that after the composing has been done the type is broken up into pages. These pages are then locked into these formes —' He pointed to a big metal frame, in which the type was locked; there were about thirty different pages of it, with blocks which made the illustrations. 'These are extremely delicate. In these formes, which contain thirty-two pages, they are placed on the machine and the machine then runs at a rate of ten thousand an hour. The printed sheets of thirty-two pages each are then folded into a section of a book. There are four sections altogether, and as this work was extremely urgent, we were using four different machines. Someone who is familiar with the work came in here last night, and unlocked the formes, and reset many of the lines by altering words and letters on several lines. The machine minders check for flaws but not for reading sense; that isn't their job. It so happened that one of them noticed acid damage on a stone – one of these tables – and examined a printed sheet more closely. It looks as if the man responsible found the task too slow, and thought of using acid, then realized that acid damage would be immediately noticeable.'

'Could it all have been done last night?' asked Roger.

'If the man knew the work, and worked very hard, yes. Some of the work has already been bound – it was an order to which we were giving absolute priority,' Sir Lancelot went on bitterly. 'Several thousands of these have already been printed, too, and that loss in itself is a very grave one. And nearly every page will have to be reset. It means that all the expense so far involved in setting the work, putting it into formes and machining, all the paper, all the ink, everything except the binding, is wasted. I would not like to compute the amount without referring to the accountants, but it is several thousand pounds. Far worse, there is the serious delay. None of these pages can be used. To put this right, a great deal – perhaps all – will have to be set on the Monotype again. You know' – he was speaking very quickly now; he gave Roger the impression that he had a blinding headache – 'that a large number of spools already set by the operators were damaged. Those spools – for other important books – were being stored because absolute priority was given to this order. This other work was delayed, and —'

He broke off.

'It will cost us three weeks' production, as well as this order,' Peter said chokily. 'Delivery was part of the contract, and we cannot now meet it.'

Roger asked: 'Does insurance cover any of this?'

'I don't know,' said Sir Lancelot. 'My co-director, Mr Richardson, handled that aspect of the business. Whether wilful damage is covered or not I cannot say. It is not the kind of risk one would expect to encounter. But we cannot insure the time. We cannot make up for the loss. It is one of the severest blows that this company could suffer, Superintendent.' He glanced up at men and women who had gathered nearer; there were fifty or sixty all within earshot, all staring at him; even the card-players were turning round and looking towards their boss. 'We shall have to stand off a considerable proportion of our staff. There will be no work in the main machine shop. There will be none in the bindery on this order – in fact, it amounts to two weeks' complete shut down, and there will be a longer period for some of the departments.'

Someone said: 'What a bloody mess.'

'And you, the police, were supposed to be watching the works,' Sir Lancelot said bitterly.

'Yes,' said Roger. 'And we were watching it.' He looked round at Tenterden. 'Who was in charge here last night, Superintendent?'

'Detective Inspector Maidment. I've sent for him,' Tenterden said. 'I've sent for all six officers who were on guard duty, Mr West, they should be here soon.'

'Six,' breathed Peter Key. 'You mean to say that you had *six* men on duty, and they allowed —' He broke off, raised his eyes towards the spidery steel girders of the roof, and added: 'And we *pay* for the police.'

'That's right,' said Roger brusquely, 'and if you paid twice as much you might get twice as many, and then we'd have a chance to do our job properly. This additional damage done with acid was the same kind of sabotage as on the spools, but acid damage at this stage would have been noticed too quickly. Is that it?'

'Yes.'

'He has ears,' muttered Peter Key.

'And it could only have been done by someone who had a thorough knowledge of the works, and knew exactly how to get at and use the formes, and reset these words by hand.'

'Yes,' said Sir Lancelot.

'Were these on the machines last night?'

'Yes.'

'So it had to be someone who was absolutely familiar with the various jobs and processes at the works.'

'Yes,' the older man answered again. 'I don't quite see —'

'I can see what he's up to,' interrupted his younger son. 'He's trying to escape responsibility by saying that it was done by one of our staff – but no one was supposed to come in here, that's what he doesn't seem to understand.'

Tenterden said: 'It would depend on what authority they had.'

'What do you mean?' flashed Peter.

'I mean that your father, or you, and probably your brother would have been able to pass the police guard, Tenterden answered stolidly.

147

'Are you suggesting that one of us—' Peter broke off, as if too angry for words.

'What Superintendent Tenterden is making obvious is that every act of sabotage in this works has been committed by someone who knows the works very well, who is familiar with the importance of and the processes of most if not all of the machines,' Roger said. 'He is also pointing out that the man or men concerned had keys. Charlie Blake's access to the keys helped to make him an obvious suspect for the first murders, and there is very little doubt that he was the most likely suspect for that very reason – he was in a position to go in and out of all of the entrances to the works freely, he knew every department, not just one or two – as most men would – and he had personal reasons for wanting to kill Jensen and his own wife. However, Blake could hardly be in a position to attack Miss Rose, or to send the car over the cliff at Bracken Head – would you agree about that, Mr Key?' He looked coldly at young Peter.

'The police hit back,' murmured Paul.

'You know damned well that it couldn't have been Blake,' retorted Peter. 'It doesn't even need saying.'

'Who else would be in quite such a convenient position?' asked Roger, still coldly. 'And who would have any reason to hate Blake enough to condemn him to his present ordeal? Who—'

He broke off, for there was a shout at a door leading to the next department. After a moment, a man screamed: *'I tell you I didn't!'* Then quite suddenly there was a crashing sound, as of breaking glass. Roger and Tenterden were the first to move, running towards the doorway. Roger was there way ahead of Tenterden, but Peter Key had made up for lost time, and was just behind him. Inside a smaller room where there were only two big machines, twenty or thirty men were rushing towards a corner, and on a platform in the corner, leading to some storage racks, stood a young man with big, dark eyes and a very pale face.

Roger recognized the van driver, but could not remember his name.

'Take the skin orf his back!' a man shouted. 'He did it all right.'

'Why don't we break his neck?'

'Come down from there, Cousins, let's see you squirm.'

148

'I tell you I didn't do it!' Cousins screamed. Roger and young Key, half-way to the back of the crowd, saw him brush the knees of his trousers, and noticed that they were ragged and torn—much as they might look if they had been burned with acid. 'I tell you I handled an empty—'

A man flung a bottle. It missed Cousins by inches, and smashed against the wall behind him. Terrified, the young man stared round at it, and as he did so, three or four men rushed forward and up the iron steps to the platform. Others sprang up to the platform, and hauled themselves on to it. Next moment, the van driver was being held by the arms and shoulders, and his trousers were being dragged off him.

'The bloody idiots,' said Peter Key. He had lost much of his resentment, his voice reminded Roger of the way he had spoken at the cars the previous day. 'Coming?' he asked, but it was a casual word, flung off without thinking. Quite suddenly he jumped forward, hauled himself up to the platform, and laid about the other young men who were man-handling Cousins. It was a magnificent sight. Man after man went staggering away, one with an elbow in his stomach, another with a fist to his nose, another with a heel on his toe. Cousins dropped heavily. Then some of the men recovered from Key's attack, but before they could do anything about it, Roger was on the platform, and Cousins was between him and young Key, who looked as if he had thoroughly enjoyed the fracas.

'Any more of this, and I'll have the lot of you inside, cooling your heels while waiting for a charge of assault,' Roger said roughly. 'What's it all about?'

'Coppers, I'd shoot 'em,' a man shouted. 'Look at his trousers! They're burned away with acid, and acid was on those formes. We ought to break his neck. Half of us will be stood off for weeks because of this.'

'I tell – I tell you I was handling an empty bottle, and it had some acid on the outside,' young Cousins almost sobbed.

'Bloody liar.'

'Why don't you arrest him?'

Roger said mildly but clearly: 'Because he didn't touch those formes last night, but we'll soon know who did. When the men who were on night duty report—'

'They were asleep.'

'Lot of sleeping beauties!'

149

'*Lot of sleeping so-and-so's, you mean.*'

Then Tenterden called quietly: 'All right, Superintendent, my men are here.'

The men on the platform shambled off. Roger led Tom Cousins down to the floor, and Peter Key brought up the rear. No one made any further attempt to attack Cousins; the arrival of more police had made most of them anxious not to cause trouble. There were four big men, including one whom Roger recognized as Detective Inspector Maidment, who had been in charge last night. The others followed him, a yard or two behind. Maidment was a spare-boned, lean-cheeked man, with a scar over his right eye. He walked with long strides, and he seemed quite unselfconscious as he reached Tenterden.

'Good morning, sir.'

' 'Morning, Maidment,' Tenterden said. 'Mr West wants to ask you a few questions about last night.'

'Very good, sir.' Maidment turned to Roger. At close quarters, it was possible to see the anxiety in his eyes, the obvious fact that he knew something had gone seriously wrong, and that it might be because he had fallen down on his job; that was probably why he was so formal. 'Good morning, Mr West.'

Roger asked quietly: 'You were in charge of the squad of police who were on duty here last night, weren't you?'

His voice carried so that everyone present heard; and now the card-players were on their feet, and men and women and girls were coming into the big shop from several entrances.

'Yes, sir,' Maidment answered.

'Do you know that a man or men entered the premises and did considerable damage?'

'So I am told, sir.'

'Do you know who came in?'

Peter Key was standing much more nonchalantly, but his chin was thrust forward, as if defying Maidment to name him. Sir Lancelot's little Van Dyck beard jutted out and up, aggressively. Paul Key was smiling the sardonic smile which seemed to be part of his expression all the time.

'Yes, sir,' said Maidment, 'and I had no authority to refuse to allow him to enter. He had the keys, too. It was Mr Sydney Richardson.'

Roger saw the consternation on every face; the astonishment on Tenterden's, even on Paul Key's. Then whispering began among the work-people, as they realized that Richardson must have been out of his mind to do this thing. It was almost an anti-climax when one of Tenterden's men came to report that Ragg and the other two men had been picked up, and that Tate had talked.

22

MOTIVE

THREE HOURS later, Roger sat in Sydney Richardson's chair behind his desk. Tenterden, Brown, and Maidment were standing at one side, the Keys were sitting on upright chairs dotted about the room. The door was closed, and two policemen stood on duty at each, to make sure that no one could come in and that no one could eavesdrop. Peter Key looked dejected and pale, his father was sitting back in a leather armchair, with Paul standing by his side; in this time of acute trouble, Paul seemed closer to his father than the other son.

'We always knew that whoever did this must have had some assistance, and we now know that three ex-criminals whom he employed were the men,' Roger said. 'I've had a statement from one man, sent to me by teletype. I'm afraid the statement makes it clear that Mr Richardson paid these men to sabotage parts of the works, at first by making the attacks appear to come from outside, so that neither he nor his hired men could be suspected. Jensen and Doris Blake disturbed them at one of these acts of sabotage, and were killed. Mr Richardson knew of the men's prison records, of course – that's why he selected them.'

Sir Lancelot said: 'It was agreed policy that ex-prisoners should be given work here and after twelve months presumed to have established themselves completely. It was Sydney's — ' He broke off.

'I'm afraid there's very little doubt, gentlemen, that Mr Richardson was responsible for the conception of the crimes, and that he set out to cause the damage and to bring the works to a standstill,' Roger said. 'But he didn't think clearly. All the evidence is that his mind was unbalanced, and that he had one obsession – a distorted desire for revenge. He did not realize that he was putting himself into the hands of the criminals he employed until he was powerless to help himself,' Roger went on. 'The murder of Jensen and Mrs Blake threw suspicion on a man whom he hated, so he found it easy to acquiesce in the murders. Then the murderers knew that they had him exactly where they wanted him.'

'I can't understand why he waited so long to – to start this revenge, if it affected him so much,' Sir Lancelot said.

'I've been discussing that on the telephone with a Home Office psychiatrist,' Roger replied. 'He assures me that delayed action in a case of repressed bitterness and resentment such as this is not uncommon – nor is the fact that when action did come, it was more violent, ruthless, and reckless. Mind you, I doubt whether we shall ever be able to establish Mr Richardson's motive strongly enough to satisfy a court, but we don't have to.'

'We all know the motive, Superintendent,' said Paul. He spoke without the slightest malicious inflection or the sardonic twist of his lips.

'Let Mr West continue,' his father said.

'In my report to my superiors, I shall submit the opinion that Mr Richardson lost his mental balance at the time of and immediately after the big strike,' Roger said. 'From that time onwards I think he was preoccupied only by one thing: avenging himself on the men whom he believed had betrayed him. He was an ideal employer, and went to extreme lengths to look after the welfare of the employees. Isn't that so, Sir Lancelot?'

Key said heavily: 'Yes, it is, Mr West. It was his whole life, and it became obsessional. When the strike came and men whom he believed he could rely on absolutely were unable to do what he thought they should, the obsession took on a different aspect. He wanted to get his own back on everyone who worked in the works. He once actually said as much, but I took no notice, I didn't dream — '

The older man broke off.

'Well, he did it,' Peter said.

After a pause, Paul said: 'Perhaps the police aren't such mutton-heads after all,' but no one took any notice of him.

'I think we shall find that Mrs Richardson had a pretty shrewd idea about this, and did her best to prevent the situation from worsening,' Roger said. 'But it got out of hand with the double murder of Jensen and Doris Blake. Blake was one of the men whom Mr Richardson believed had betrayed him. He had allowed an *affaire* to flourish at the works between Blake's wife and the night-watchman, Jensen.' Roger glanced

153

at Tenterden. 'No normal employer would have allowed that; it was the first indication that Richardson wasn't simply being driven off his head with anxiety, but that he had a malicious streak. To protect his hired men, he had to allow Blake to be charged and might have kept silent had Blake been convicted. The man Tate's statement says that Rose Richardson began to make inquiries which were bound to lead to the truth – it would be fatal for anyone so close to Richardson to start probing. So Tate and his two accomplices kidnapped her, to make sure that she didn't find out too much. One man says that he thought the kidnapping was simply to make her talk, but there isn't much doubt that they meant to kill her. As her father had already acquiesced in two murders, they thought it certain that they could make him endure this. His only alternative was to be branded with the truth. Knowing the men, I think it probable that they convinced him that he would be thought guilty of conniving at his daughter's murder. We now know that in fact the attack on his daughter drove Mr Richardson to final desperation, a last act of sabotage, and suicide,' Roger finished. 'I don't think Tate and his accomplices expected this. I do know now that they expected Miss Richardson's car to sink under the sea, thus drowning her – in fact, Tate himself admits that he reached inside Mr Soley's car and released the hand-brake. There is another interesting side issue,' Roger went on, as if anxious to relieve the tension a little. 'Soley was not only an obvious suspect to us, but an obvious one to Tate and his men. They used to borrow Soley's car occasionally, and actually had it on the night of the attack on Miss Richardson. It served exactly the purpose they wanted – threw suspicion on Mr Soley.'

'Thank God Sydney's dead,' Sir Lancelot said gruffly.

Peter said jerkily: 'If you had my uncle in mind, Mr West, why didn't you have him watched, to make sure that he couldn't do more damage, and couldn't kill himself? I disagree with my father; it would have been more just if Mr Richardson had stood trial.'

'Until we knew that he had come here last night we had no indication of the truth,' Roger said. 'Mrs Richardson's refusal to tell us all she could, Miss Richardson's reluctance to talk, and the great difficulty we had in trying to make Mr Richardson go into details all pointed to the one thing; the suicide made it evident. I didn't know that Mr Richardson went from

Kemble to the works, and then home. His wife told me that he came straight home and went to bed. She strove to the last moment to try to help him. He'd told her a pack of lies to explain his behaviour and his fears, and I think she pretended to believe them. She told me she did, being so anxious to protect him.'

'Yes,' said Sir Lancelot, 'I can understand how Mary would believe him, and how loyal she would be. And to think — ' He broke off.

'My father was about to say that as a family we always disapproved of Mary Richardson,' put in Paul heavily. 'It was decreed that Uncle Sydney, as we called him, married beneath him. How snobbish can you get? There isn't any danger of her being involved, is there?'

'Not unless new and unexpected evidence turns up,' said Roger. He stood up, studied the three men for a few seconds, then looked at Tenterden and said: 'We'd better get off, Arthur. Let me know if there is anything else you want, gentlemen.' He went off briskly, and got into Tenterden's car.

A crowd of workers was hovering about the gates, and a man on a soap box was saying in a loud voice:

'It's always the same, the first to suffer are the workers. They needn't stand a single one of us off, and what I say is, if they stand a single one of us off the rest of us ought to down tools until everyone's reinstated. They've got plenty of money . . .'

The car moved out of earshot. Tenterden turned down the road towards Corby, passing the spot where Doris Blake had first sensed trouble. The Corby man drove slowly, and halfway towards the town he said:

'When do you think we ought to have Blake up at another hearing, Handsome? We'll offer no evidence, and the quicker he's free, the better.'

'I'd call an early court tomorrow,' Roger said. 'Ragg and the others will be here by then – we can charge 'em at the same time.'

Tenterden said: 'I'll fix it as soon as I get back. There's another thing, Handsome. I ought to make my wife go and eat humble pie before Sam Soley.'

'Sam needn't know he was seriously suspected,' Roger said solemnly.

'Women!' said Brown.

155

'Did you expect Richardson to kill himself?' Tenterden demanded.

'I suppose I ought to admit that it didn't surprise me,' Roger said, 'but it's easy to have hindsight. What matters now is trying to make sure that the harm he did doesn't spread. They could have a lot more labour trouble at the works, and it might become chronic. If Sir Lancelot Key's got any sense, he'll get Rose Richardson there as soon as the hospital and Arnold will let her go. One appearance would be a good idea. And if I were the Keys I'd take Paul back into the business and turn him on to the Ministry to agree to hold those text-books orders back. I'd stand the men off at half rate, or else find them something to do. Richardson always said that Sir Lancelot and Peter Key were useless with the workers. Paul might be better.'

Tenterden was smiling.

'If I know Rose, when she hears what's happened she'll go to the works if she has to be carried on a stretcher. And if Sir Lancelot talks about standing anyone off, she'll tell him what she thinks of him. I must say Paul was a surprise to me. Got more about him than I ever thought. May have learned his lesson, and want to get back into the business. There's another thing, too – now Richardson's gone, Paul and Rose might get together again.'

'You never know,' said Brown.

They pulled up outside the police station, hurried up to Tenterden's office, and were met by the man who looked rather like Salmon, and who said eagerly:

'There's a message in from the Yard, sir. Mr Cope said that there isn't anything to worry about, Carter's made a statement, too. All three men will be here by eight o'clock in the morning.'

Tenterden said: 'That's just what we wanted to hear, Harry. Now, you go round and see your sister-in-law and your mother. No need to come in again until after the funeral.'

The other said: 'Thanks very much, sir.' He turned to Roger, hesitated, and then said quietly: 'I hope you won't mind if I thank you for risking your life to try to save my brother's. We'll always remember it.'

He put out his hand.

Rose Richardson was looking pale but bright-eyed when she reached the works late the next morning. Paul had driven her from the home of her friend, where she had been staying.

According to the report Roger received afterwards, she spent ten minutes with Sir Lancelot and Peter Key, then came out and announced that if it were necessary to stand anybody off, it would be at half pay. By then, the Composing Room was working at full pressure, stand-by jobs were being run off the machines, and the works had regained the appearance of bustling activity.

Roger stayed the night in Corby, telephoned Janet a little after nine, and went to bed early. He was up at seven next morning, and at the court by eight, when Blake was formally discharged and Ragg, Carter, and Tate charged. Roger went on to the works. Rose Richardson was already there, and the moment she saw Roger she asked:

'How long will it be before Charlie Blake is back at work, Mr West?'

'He'll be home today, anyhow,' Roger said.

'I hope you'll advise him to come straight here,' said Rose. 'It will do him good, and heaven knows we need him.'

Blake was back at the works by eleven o'clock.

'I can't say I give you full marks for that case, Dad,' Scoopy West said, that evening. 'You might at least have kept those machines from running for a fortnight, when we might have had a few days without text-books. Richardson and Key print half of ours.'

'Don't you believe it,' said Richard. 'They'd give us some old dog-eared things just to keep our noses stuck to the print.' His eyes were glowing. 'Dad, you ought to have been at school this afternoon, your ears would have burned. I think every chap had something to say about the way you tried to rescue the detective, Salmon. I know one thing, I'm jolly proud to be a son of yours. Aren't I, Scoop?'

Martin-called-Scoopy looked straight into his father's eyes, and said: 'I certainly am.'

'When all the mush is over, you boys can help lay the table,' Janet said. 'I read the papers too, and all I can say is that I'd rather have a live husband than a dead hero.'

'We've heard that old stuff before,' jeered Scoopy. 'You wouldn't have Dad any different, and nor would we. Was it one of the better cases, Dad?'

'Depends how you mean,' said Roger. 'It's one I nearly muffed badly, and never mind why. If I hadn't, we might

157

have finished the inquiry earlier, and we might have saved a life.'

Janet said, almost crossly: 'You're never satisfied, are you?'

It was a week later when Roger had a lettter from Maggie Tenterden, saying that she hoped he would bring his wife and the boys to Corby for a few days in the Easter holidays. He jumped at the chance, and Tenterden arranged an invitation from Rose Richardson to take the family round the works. When Roger drove between the gates he saw round-faced Gordon, saluting him. In Richardson's office, Paul Key came forward to welcome the party. Rose soon joined them, looking almost gay, certainly pleased to see them. She took them round the works, where every Monotype machine was click-click-clicking away, the two Linotypes were busy, the spools were whirling on the Monotype casting machines. In the big machine shop, the flat-bed machines were humming, the huge rotaries were flying round. Beyond these, the girls were busy at the binding machines, everything was working at full pressure. Charlie Blake was working on the erection of a new colour-printing flat-bed, and looked younger and arrestingly handsome. He shook hands warmly, then went back to his job.

'How did the text-book order go?' asked Roger.

'Oh, Paul fixed it,' Rose said, and glanced at Paul Key, who was talking to the guillotine minder. Richard and Scoopy watched fascinated as the guillotine blade sliced off the edges of the books.

'Gossip says Rose and Paul are getting married at Whitsun,' Tenterden announced, when they had left the works. 'The place is different altogether, Handsome. Richardson's death was like the lifting of a shadow. His widow's twice the woman she was, too.' He lowered his voice. 'I've often thought about it, Handsome. If we'd caught Richardson in time and he'd had to stand trial I doubt whether the works would ever have been quite the same again. If it weren't for poor Salmon, I'd say that everything worked out for the best. Salmon's wife's taking in boarders, you know. Charlie Blake's given up his cottage and lives at her place.' After a pause, he added: 'Can't have everything, I suppose.'

'I suppose not,' echoed Roger heavily.

THESE ARE  PAN BOOKS

Dianne Doubtfire

REASON FOR VIOLENCE

Since early childhood Pauletta was captive to the evil influence of her cousin Gilbert. His diabolical use of it was to lead to inevitable tragedy. 'The chiller of the season' – *Bristol Evening Post*.   (3/6)

Dianne Doubtfire

LUST FOR INNOCENCE

Chosen by *Books and Bookmen* as 'the best first novel of 1960', this is the suspense-filled story of a guilt-ridden child who became a man's prey. 'A novel of cruelty and horror, yet also of warmth and understanding' – *New York Times* (2/6)

PICK OF THE PAPERBACKS

PAN books

Publication May 8th

THE RISE AND FALL OF THE THIRD REICH

by William L. Shirer

A famous bestseller in hardback at 70/-

NOW ONLY **12'6** (U.K.)